I0552500

In The Shadow of a Substitute Son

PAULETTE BERNARD

DEDICATION

This book is dedicated to my daughter Meagan Montanez who is always challenging me to write the next masterpiece, and to my family, who inspires me every day with tenacity and drive that helps me pursue my writing dream. I am proud to be part of an artistic family. To my husband, who loves me although he does not understand my weirdness.

CONTENTS

ACKNOWLEDGMENTS

Thanks to my family and friends for their continued support as I continue my literary journey. To all the writers who have published a book that inspired me to you, I say "Thank You."

1 THE BEGINNING

On October 16, 1967, a young man named Michael Grayeson II was born 6 lbs. 11 oz. and eight inches long in weight and height. His father was ecstatic to have someone who would continue his legacy. Michael Sr. was 6' 9", large in stature, with fair skin, large brown eyes with a short haircut, and a very forceful man on the football field. Ever since he was a young man, Michael Grayeson has tried to build a successful professional football career. Sadly, his health sidelined him after one-year playing college football. His love for the game caused him to change his passion from playing to coaching.

The birth of his son gave Michael Sr. a renewed chance for a Grayeson to have a professional football career. Michael Grayeson II, who lay in his mother's arms crying like every other newborn baby, had no way of knowing the plans for his future made instantly by his father. Although the baby was new to the world, his father noticed the exceptional size of his hands. Seeing the outstretched fingers of his pale son as he moved them around to grab his mother's finger gave the father hope that his son would follow him.

The baby cried and cooed as his little face searched for food. The nurses and doctors laughed as it is customary for the newborns to go to the nursery first. The OB/GYN doctor nodded to the new mother to give her permission to feed the baby. Moments later, the nurse whisked little Michael off to the nursery. Laverne Grayeson was 5'11" with almond-shaped brown eyes and caramel-color skin. She was very slender even though she carried her baby to the full term of her pregnancy.

Laverne struggled with bulimia throughout her life which aided in the lack of body fat she exhibits. The unexpected pregnancy of her son gave her renewed strength to change her eating habits. She sought treatment from her nutritionist and OB/GYN throughout her pregnancy. Laying in the bed, she could see how proud her husband was to have a son, yet she also saw an unusual expression on his face which caused her some concern. Something about holding her son pushed an overwhelming protective sensation in her body and caused her emotions to be alerted.

Looking at her husband, she asked, "what are you thinking?" She feared his focus would be more on football than on his son. Michael Sr. gazed at his wife and replied, "I did not get a chance to show the world how good I was, but now my son will get that chance. The Grayeson name will reign once again in the football circuit."

Laverne knew her fears were slowly manifesting into reality. She opened her arms as a gesture toward her husband. He leaned over and hugged her and gave her a little squeeze. Using the intimate moment, she whispered, "football may be your dream, but it may not be his." As a husband, Michael understood his wife was protecting them, yet as a father, he wants his namesake to love what he loves. What he loved most of all was playing football.

As the days turned into years, Michael Sr. began showing young Michael his football pictures, high school trophies, and his junior year MVP award. He was proud of his achievement but kept replaying his asthma attack on the field during the first grade in his sophomore year, which caused the doctor to rule him ineligible to play. Michael II wanted to understand more about asthma than football.

2 NEW FRIENDSHIPS

Michael Sr. developed a routine that includes playing football every Saturday. At 4'11" and 110 pounds, Michael II practiced with the local teams or watched from the sidelines. The young man tried his best to please his father, but he had no interest or passion for playing the sport. He focused on the game's athleticism and the human body's ability to endure pain.

One Saturday in September, as he sat on the sidelines watching his father's and the opposing teams play, he became intrigued with the players' movement. He recalled how they moved differently in the fall versus the summer. He became excited to see how they play during the winter. He developed an increased passion for the medical field at an early age. Mr. Grayeson grew increasingly unhappy with his son's lack of drive for his beloved sport.

The Grayeson family gathered every night for dinner. The conversation decreased between father and son as Michael II began inquiring more about the effects of asthma, not the football field's positions. The unhappy father began to vocalize his displeasure and disappointment with his son's refusal to understand the game's premise. Laverne Grayeson understandably hoped her husband could achieve his dream through his son, but she encouraged him to follow his passion as a mother. The bond between mother and son grew stronger.

Michael II attended public school with his cousin Robert Denningson. The boys did not have many friends in the first few months of school. In the middle of his seventh-grade semester,

Michael noticed Larry Martin's weird eating habit in the cafeteria. The last Friday before the winter break, Michael watched Larry, who was shy, eating half his sandwich while putting the other half and an apple in a small bag. Michael sensed something was wrong, and out of curiosity, he asked, "why are you putting the food in your bag? Aren't you hungry?" The question startled Larry because he had not expected Michael to speak to him. Nevertheless, he answered honestly, "if I eat it all now, I won't have anything to eat tonight."

Larry was a couple of inches shorter than Michael but was very skinny. His long greasy hair and ill-fitted clothes depict the lack of care he was receiving. Hearing his response, Michael felt saddened in his heart. Even though he did not know the entire story, he knew the young man had more to say about the situation. He asks, "Why wouldn't you have anything to eat tonight? Isn't your mother going to cook dinner?" The inquisitor could not understand a child not having a home cook meal. A sincere Larry answered, "no, my mom does not cook. She works at night, I think, because she leaves as soon as I get home from school, and she is asleep when I leave in the morning. I think we must move soon, though, because I heard her yelling at a man about needing more time to find a new apartment. The man yelled back she had until the end of the month. When I woke up this morning, she was not there." He shrugged his shoulder without concern when he finished.

The thought of his schoolmate living alone at such an immature age terrified Michael. The bell rang before he could respond, sounding the end of their lunch break. Throughout the remainder of the day, the terrible visions of his classmate plagued Michael's mind. Finally, the last bell rang, and as the children piled into the narrow hallway, Michael searched for Larry. He spotted him walking out of the side door toward the bus stand. Running past the other students, he yelled out Larry's name to gain his attention. Larry turned to find the person calling his name and saw Michael. He stopped to give his classmate a chance to catch up to him. Almost breathless, Michael spoke, "Hey, do you want to come to my house for dinner?" Larry was a little skeptical because he did not know Michael, but the growl in his stomach betrayed him. "Is your mother cooking?" He asked as a way of returning the question from earlier. Smiling at his new friend, Michael replied, "yes, my mom cooks every night, so do you want to come over?" The hungry youngster felt a little jealous of the answer as he replied in agreement. Feeling at peace, Larry walked with Michael to meet his mother at the car pickup location.

3 THE INTRODUCTION

Trekking across the schoolyard towards the car, Michael II began rehearsing his introduction of Larry to his mother. On impulse, the young man extended a dinner invitation to Larry. He allowed the terrifying images he imagined in his mind to overshadow the possibility his parents may not be as receptive. Seeing his mother's Silver Mitsubishi Outlander pulling up to the sidewalk, Michael grabbed Larry's arm and began running.

The young man was slightly out of breath when he opened the back passenger side door to greet his mother. "Hi momma, this is Larry. Can he come to our house for dinner? His mother does not cook, and he is alone at the house." Speaking rapidly, Michael pulled Larry into the car as he climbed into the back seat. Laverne turned her head and looked at the young man, who appeared very malnourished, then nodded in agreement.

The concerned mother drove home as soon as the passenger door closed. Although she agreed to have him over for dinner, Laverne wanted to learn more about the young man. "Hello, Larry. How are you doing?" she asked. It was the first time an adult, besides his teacher, spoke directly to him.

Holding his head down, Larry answered, "I am hungry, ma'am," because he did not understand the question. Mrs. Grayeson smiled at the young man's honesty but recognized he lacked conversation etiquette. Michael, in excitement, began talking about all the things he wanted to show Larry when they got home. Half listening to his classmate, Larry looked out the car at the large houses. They were much nicer than the buildings in his neighborhood.

As the family pulled into the driveway and the garage door opened, Larry squealed unconsciously, "wow, you have an actual garage. I have never driven into a garage before." His comment caused Laverne's left eyebrow to rise. "Where has this boy been living?" She asked herself.

Michael exited the car and yelled for Larry to come into the house to show him his room. Larry felt envious of his classmate as he followed behind him. "Don't forget to wash your hands," Laverne called after them as she walked from the garage into the small hallway leading to the open living and dining area. She put her bag on the chair and pulled out the grilled chicken, lettuce, tomatoes, and bread to make the boys a sandwich before dinner.

Michael rushed into the bathroom, washed his hands, and motioned Larry to do the same. Completing his mandatory task, he walked into his bedroom. Standing at the door, the size of the room felt significant to Larry, who shared a room with his mother. "Is this all your space?" He asked Michael.

A strange look appeared on Michael's face since he had engaged in a real conversation with Larry for the first time. The question felt odd, but he answered nonetheless. "Yes, this is my room. My parent's room is down the hall, and we have two extra rooms at the other end for when family visits." Larry looked in amazement around the young boy's room. Saddened by his current home life, he tried to put a smile forward in front of Michael.

"Boys, it's time to eat," Laverne called out to the boys. Michael ran out of the room towards the kitchen, Larry following close behind him. Approaching the table, Larry saw the sandwich with chips and juice on the table. "Is this dinner?" He asked. Michael quickly responds, "no way, it's our snack before dinner.".

Snack before dinner was another strange concept for Larry. He typically eats the fruit he brought from school while waiting to eat the other half of his sandwich or whatever food he takes home for dinner. Sitting at the table, he watched Michael and copied everything he did, including blessing his food before eating. Although he did not know what to say, he mumbled, "thank you, Lord, for the food, Amen."

Laverne took the opportunity to learn a little more about this young man. "Larry, what is your last name?" She asked softly. Putting the sandwich on the plate, he answered. "My last name is Martin, ma'am." Mrs. Grayeson smiled at his politeness. She suspects the young man's short life had not been easy. Pulling out the chair, she sat down to not look intimidating to him. "Tell me about yourself, Mr. Martin." She told him.

Larry looked puzzled at the woman sitting across from him. Before finishing his sandwich, he did not know what to tell her, so he gave her the basic, "my name is Larry Martin, and I am 12 years old." It became clear to Michael's mother that she must ask poignant questions to Larry.

After several minutes and various questions, Laverne learned that Larry lived with his mother, who was often absent from his life during the critical time of the day and did not know his father. She also learned he only visited the clinic to get the required immunization for school and did not remember going to a dentist. Not wanting him to be uncomfortable, Laverne forgoes any more questions. Leaving the boys to finish their snack, she retreated to the kitchen to start dinner.

Michael Sr., a coach at the local high school, drove home from practice feeling deflated. Parking in his driveway, he remained in the vehicle for twenty minutes. Reflecting on how the fathers and sons interacted at training made him wish his son would be more active in the sport. Finally, he exited the vehicle to join his family in the house.

He saw Larry, a skinny boy, admiring his football plagues on the wall, walking through the door. "Hey, who are you?" He asked. At 4'5" and 65 pounds, Larry was tiny compared to Michael Sr., a 6'9" 200-pound man. The panic-stricken boy looked frightened at the large man in front of him. "I am Larry." His words tremble as he answers the question. Laverne quickly stepped in to explain that Larry was their dinner guest. Michael Sr. asked, "you like football?" Still shaking, Larry responded, "I love football, sir."

4 THE SUBTLE SHIFT

The party streamers flew around the room; the kazoos sound traveled throughout the house, signaling the ending of another year. "Happy New Year," the Grayeson family shouted with other family members and friends to celebrate a new decade.

After seeing his home life, Laverne Grayeson, a psychiatrist by trade, petitioned the court to become Larry Martin's legal guardian. Although the court could not find the young boy's mother, the Judge decided to grant temporary guardianship to the family. The decision was bitter-sweet for Michael's future relationship with his father. However, in the present moment, a new year meant new birthday celebrations for the two boys after discovering they share the same date of birth and birth year.

The New Year also meant a new job for Michael Sr., who accepted the Director of Athletic Performance position at Cedar Valley University. Not only did he obtain a salary increase, but he had an opportunity to become more submerged in the sport he loved. Being a supportive wife, Laverne was happy but concerned about his football obsession.

As the festivities dwindled, the family returned their focus to planning for the New Year. The boys were excited about Michael Sr. being part of college football, but for varied reasons. Young Michael dreams about seeing the medical team caring for the older players. Larry, who secretly desired to be a wide receiver, wanted to be part of the environment to meet the players he watched on their local television.

Later in the evening, while sitting around the mahogany brown extended dining table, Michael tried to talk about football with his father. "Daddy, when you start working at the school, are you going to run on the sidelines like the guys we see on TV?" Surprised by his son's question, the father immediately had a glimmer of hope that the young man was gaining a passion for the sport. "Son, I will be helping the players to make sure they are fit to play the game. I'll be on the sidelines watching and monitoring their performance but don't think there'll be much running for your old man." Mr. Grayeson answered with pride.

"So, working with the player means you have an important job, right?" Young Michael asked his father.

The older gentleman pondered his son's question for a few minutes before responding. "I guess you can say my job is important. You boys can come down when you are out of school and watch me work."

Looking at each other in excitement, the boys knew being in the big stadium was significant. "I always wish I could play in the game, but I don't have the skills to play," Larry mumbled. His words penetrated the core of Michael Sr.'s brain. He immediately stopped eating and looked at the young man. "Son," he started, "you want to play football?"

Larry felt joy in his heart hearing someone calling him a son. Quickly he answered, "yes, I love the game, but I didn't have anyone to teach me how to play, so I never learned."

The older man sat back in his chair and clapped his large hands three times before rubbing them together in excitement. "Junior, you hear what he said? He wants to play football. What do you think about that?" He said to Larry, "Son, we can fix that issue; I can help you. We can start with the lessons on the game tomorrow. It will be a pleasure to teach you, son." Just like that, the shift in dynamics changed.

Michael Sr. began calling Larry 'son' every chance he got and referred to Michael as 'junior.' Laverne recognized the change immediately and looked at her husband with stern eyes. Even if it was temporary, Mr. Grayeson was too excited about a family member wanting to play football to notice his wife's facial expression.

The days turned into weeks and then months. Michael Sr. and Larry spent hours practicing the running back, quarterback, and wide receiver's positions on the offensive side of the game. They also discussed various parts of the game on the defensive side and the processes. He entrusted training to one of his closest friends on his busy days. Michael asked to join numerous times, and his father occasionally would say no or ignore him. Michael Sr. focused on his new job and Larry's football progress.

Mrs. Grayeson knew football was important to her son even though it differed from her husband's. She would take Michael to the university countless times after school to watch his father work with the students. Sadly, Michael Sr. never acknowledges his son's visits. Fortunately, on one of those visits, he met Dr. Thelia Brown.

The young boy had not seen a female sports doctor before meeting her, so he was intrigued. Dr. Brown recognized the same passion in the young man she had when she was his age and took an interest in him. After speaking to Laverne, she offered to give Michael the guidance he needed to study orthopedic medicine. Michael found a new role model and forgot about his father's impressive job.

The job was going better than expected, the children were approaching high school, and Laverne restarted her practice. Everything was going perfectly well for the family when Laverne received a letter notifying her of Larry's mother's petition to vacate the temporary guardianship order from two years prior. Immediately, Mrs. Grayeson contacted her husband to inform him of the situation. Michael Sr. saw his dreams of having a football star evaporate instantly.

5 A MOTHER'S DILEMMA

"No, No, No!" Michael Sr. shouted as he threw the clipboard against the wall. The loud bang of the clipboard hitting the wall frightened the students in the locker room. "You okay, coach?" One of the students inquired. "Yeah, I am. I just got some unexpected news. We are done for today, so grab your stuff and clear out." The upset father responded. The students, thrilled with an early dismissal from training, gathered their items and rushed out.

Michael Sr. went back to his office and sat for another ten minutes. As the thought of his dreams diminishing with Larry's removal increased, so did his anger. He grabbed his keys and drove home at top speed.

Meanwhile, after hearing the news, Laverne sensed that her husband would not work. Instantly she decided to spare the children from the negative conversation by removing them from the house before her husband arrived.

Scrolling through her phonebook, she called her friend Stephanie and asked her to take the kids out for pizza with her son. Offering to pay was a good incentive to ensure her friend would comply. After Stephanie left with the kids, Michael Sr. pulled into the driveway. Sitting in the car, he banged his hand on the steering wheel several times in disapproval of the petition.

Finally stepping out of the vehicle, he closed the door so hard it caused the windows in his Chevy Suburban to shake. Hearing the noise, Laverne prepared herself for the storm she called a husband. "Hi sweetheart, before you start ranting and raving, let's take a deep breath." She spoke aloud as Michael Sr. walked around the corner from the small hallway into the living area.

"How can you be so calm? You know they are trying to take my son, right?" He snapped at his wife. Shaking her head, his wife responds, "they are not trying to take your son," in a soft voice. Larry's mother asked the Judge to return him to her. We knew he was only here temporarily."

The words "they are not trying to take your son" should have caused the large man to pause and think. However, it pushed Michael Sr. over the edge. Panting extremely hard, he paced back and forth to formulate his words. "What do you mean he is not my son? He has been with us for the past two years, so he is my son. The only thing left to do is adopt him legally and change his name." The man began rambling with many suggestions to find some solution to the problem.

Laverne, who had enough of her husband's childish behavior, stood to her feet and yelled at him. "Michael Salomon Grayeson, stop it right now. It would be best to calm down to discuss this like two rational people. Yelling and screaming will not solve the issue. Sit down and listen." The sternness in her voice caused her husband to stop walking and look at her.

Mr. Grayeson had been so focused on losing the young boy that he lost sight of everything else. "You are right, honey. I'm sorry." Sitting on the sofa, Michael patted the space next to him for her to join him. "What are we going to do?" He asked calmly.

For the first time in Michael Sr.'s life, he felt helpless. His entire future now depends on his wife's ability to keep Larry in the family. The sympathetic look on her husband's face troubled Laverne. She knew he invested much time and effort into Larry, but it was for selfish reasons. On the other hand, she must consider what was best for Larry's future. Handing the letter to her husband, she replies, "the letter says she made a petition. It did not say the Judge overturned the decision. First, let us find out more about our options, then we can agree on the best direction for Larry's sake."

The disappointed father took the letter and reread it. He slowly understood what his wife was telling him. "Did you call George?" He asked. Before responding, Laverne took her husband's hand, "yes, I called George. He is the one with the law degree. We should hear something back tomorrow after he reached out to the court." She told him in a soft tone.

Stephanie received an emergency page from work in the middle of pizza time. It meant she had to bring the children home earlier than expected. Although she wanted to call Laverne to notify her of the change, she had to remain focused on the issues with her job. Michael II and Larry hopped out of the car and ran into the house. The older Michael neglected to close the door when he arrived earlier in his excitement. As soon as they walked into the house, both boys heard Michael Sr. ask his wife, "why do you think his mother wants him back now?" The news of his mother stirred up mixed emotions in the young boy. "Did you say my mother is back?" He asked with a quizzical look on his face.

Stunned by the boy's comment, the adults stopped talking because they did not expect them to be in the house. Michael Sr. mistook Larry's confused facial expression as rejecting the idea of returning to his mother.

"That is our assumption because of the letter we receive. You okay with that?" Michael Sr. asked.

"I don't know?" Larry responded.

"Are you going to leave us?" Michael II asked the young man he grew to consider his brother. Perplexed by the thought of her husband neglecting his son and Michael losing someone he felt was family, Laverne tried to find the right words. The protective mother posed a simple question to Larry, "don't you miss your mother?"

The question was overwhelming for the boy. Seeing him struggle with the answer, she encouraged him to speak freely. "I miss her, but I don't want to leave you all because I love it here. Is that wrong?" He asked shyly.

Mrs. Grayeson walked over to the boys and hugged them. As a mother, she did not feel comfortable keeping a child from his biological parent. The complexity of the situation concerns how her husband treats his son. Allowing Larry to stay only means Michael Sr. will continue to alienate his biological son. "There is nothing wrong with wanting to stay because it means we are doing our job as guardians. I will not lie to you; we do not know the situation with your mother. I can promise you that once we get more details, we will share them with you and allow you to make a choice. How does that sound?" She told him before walking to the kitchen.

The boys nodded in agreement and then ran to their rooms. Michael Sr. suspected his wife might not be as eager for Larry to remain with them. As her husband, he could not understand it but was determined to make her see his point of view. The worried man suspects his wife could side with Larry's mother and send him back. Still sitting on the sofa, he began to strategize.

6 GIVE ME BACK MY SON

Family law was not George Bronston's career choice when he graduated from law school six months before meeting Laverne Grayeson. Through an introduction by his mother, George sat in her living room listening to Laverne's concern for her son's classmate.

Although he was not confident in family court cases, he contacted friends, read various case laws, and spent time in the law library before submitting the motion to the court. Four months later, the Judge's decision changed his legal journey. Now a full-time family advocate, he immediately reached out to the court when he learned about the petition.

Sidney Washington was a tall, slender, beautiful girl with dreams of becoming an actor and a singer. Leaving her parents' home at seventeen, she felt confident in achieving her goals until she met Amelia Gooderson. Amelia was charming and full of promises. She met the young woman at the airport and admired her spunk, physique, and smile. Amelia learned enough about the young girl to guide the chat her way during their conversation. By the time they boarded the plane, the older woman had convinced the naïve young woman to attend a party with her.

During the party, Sidney met several affluent clients whom Amelia promised would help expose her to top producers. Her innocence and beauty drew many of the older men's attention. She enjoyed many compliments, but before she knew it, Amelia consumed her life. From the outside, attending parties, going on trips, and staying in fancy hotels seemed fun. However, much more was expected from the women in Exceptional Personal Services.

From the age of seventeen to thirty-five, Sidney was Amelia's darling. Now at thirty-five, Sidney was pregnant. Her pregnancy meant she was no longer attractive or valuable to Amelia. As soon as the evidence of the pregnancy was visible, Amelia ended her association with Sidney. Miss Washington, who resided at one of Amelia's properties, had never lived on her own or rented an apartment before. With little money and a baby on the way, she settled for a cheap studio apartment in the rougher part of the city.

Part of Amelia's strategy was to alienate the ladies from their families. Leaving the comforts of Amelia's home, the pregnant mother attempted to contact her family. Her attempts failed because she was unaware of her parents' medical tragedy over the past years. At last, she found her sister's information, but Sandra refused to have any contact with her. This rejection meant she had no one to turn to.

Sidney began suffering from depression and early signs of schizophrenia right after Larry was born. With no college degree or essential work-life skills, the young mother could not find employment. After rejection from several job aspects, she got a job at the local supermarket. When Larry turned six, his mother met a young man who recognized her from the past and connected her with another gentleman who began taking her out to expensive restaurants and risky parties.

Their arrangements lasted four years before ending suddenly. Finding herself in the same studio apartment with her son, she tried to make the money she got from her companion stretch. She also worked odd jobs until she found a night job in a new warehouse across town. It was tough, but she did her best to stay positive until the property owner left an eviction notice on her door. Because she was never late on her rent, the eviction surprised her and retriggered her schizophrenia.

During one of those episodes at work, the doctor hospitalized her in the psychiatric ward. Upon arrival at the hospital, Sidney kept inquiring about her son. She informed the hospital staff her son was home alone, but they did not believe her. The hospital alerted the police, who visited the home to do their due diligence. Unfortunately, Larry was having dinner at the Grayeson's house when they arrived. His absence led them to believe she imagined her son.

Two years later, the doctor cleared her to leave the hospital.

Immediately, she began searching for Larry. After speaking with a social worker, they discovered the young man was placed in a temporary guardianship with the Grayeson family. Crying uncontrollably before the social worker, Sidney kept repeating, "give me back my son." Her cries broke the social worker's heart so much that she asked her lawyer friend, Richard Pickerton, to take the case pro bono.

Following his conversation with the social worker, Richard's first task was to vacate the guardianship. Knowing her hospitalization would be a factor, he placed it upfront in the petition and created a plan of action for the young mother to protect her son. Richard and George met to discuss the case. Both men suspect it could be a bitter fight at the end of the meeting.

George contacted Laverne to update her on Larry's mother. Hearing about her situation was heartbreaking, but it made Mrs. Grayeson wonder if Larry would be safe with her. The more the conversation progressed, the tougher her decision became.

7 LET THE BATTLE BEGIN

The heavy footsteps of Michael Sr. got drowned out by the Pilate teacher's instruction on the television. He smiled at his wife as she stretched because her body still excites him. "Hey sexy," he spoke, kissing the back of her sweaty neck. Laverne finished her stretching before responding to her husband. "Hey sweetie, you are early today."

The dutiful husband put his bag and phone on the little table in the corner of the room. Walking into the kitchen, he pulled out a beer from the fridge and sat on the black-armed bar stool at the white marbled quartz kitchen island. "It was a smooth day today. Did you hear back from George?" He questioned.

The question confused his wife. Since they met, she had never lied to him, and now she is in an uncomfortable position. If she tells him about Sidney's past, he will use it to keep Larry, but it can negatively impact her marriage if she does not. In the end, she recounted what she heard from George.

"Are you telling me his mother is a hooker?" He whispered, thinking the boys were in their rooms.

Laverne tried to add class to the woman's previous work classification. "No, he said she was an escort to wealthy men."

Michael placed the beer on the counter, slid his bottom to the end of the stool, and slightly leaned forward. "It doesn't matter if they gave her $10 or ten grand; it is still hooking. My Larry does not need to be around that. I am sure we will have no problem keeping him with us." His face was beaming with joy at the news.

Mrs. Grayeson was not surprised by her husband's response. Shaking her head, she slapped his leg before going to their bedroom suite to take a shower.

Meanwhile, back at the law firm of Pickerton & Chadwicks, Esqs., the pressure of reuniting a mother and son is building. The biggest hurdle for the older lawyer was Sidney's previous employment and hospitalization. Part of his tactic was to perform extensive research on Laverne and Michael Grayeson, but his team did not find much information. Asking his PI to dig more, he focused on finding a Judge who did not put much thought into a woman's career choice.

After twenty years of practicing law, he built up a lengthy list of favors with court staff. His first task was to contact the court to push for a date. Slipping into his office, he called his friend Janice Barley. "Hi Janice, it's Richard."

"Richard Pickerton, it has been a minute since we have seen you. Where have you been?" Janice responded.

"I am still here but grooming my son to take over when I retire," Richard told her.

"Wow, so it is true that you are considering retirement. Glad to hear it. What can I do for you then?" She asked.

"I need to get a case before Judge Martin Canister as soon as possible. Can you make that happen for me?" He asked while leaning back in his large brown leather chair.

"Let me look at his calendar." After a few minutes, she returned to the phone. "The earliest date I can give you is three weeks from now. Do you want it?" Janice asked while searching for the case number.

Richard had no choice but to accept the date. He knew it was his client's only chance to overcome her past issues against the guardianship family. He replied, "we'll take it." putting his feet on the desk.

On the other hand, at Bronston, Esq., George felt confident about his child's mother's information. Because he was sure his client would get full custodial custody of the boy, he decided to use her medical condition to prove her home would be unsafe for a child.

As the court battle gears up between the legal teams, so did the fight for a dad's attention at the Grayeson home. After drinking his beer, Michael Sr. noticed how extremely quiet the house was. "Where are the boys?" He shouted at his wife while she finished redressing.

Walking back into the living room, Laverne responded, "they went with Mark to the football field." Entering the kitchen, she picked up the small towel off the counter. Laverne started gathering food to make dinner while listening to her husband. Shocked at her response, Michael Sr. remarked, "Junior went too. I thought he did not like football?"

Upset about her husband's comment, Laverne slammed the towel against the counter, "Michael Grayeson, did you forget he is your biological son?"

"Woman, I know he is my son; I'm shocked he wanted to join them at practice." He responded.

"He went because he loves football just as much as you do but in a separate way. You know he wants to be an orthopedic doctor treating athletes, right. What do you think about that?" She asked him in a cynical tone.

Michael Sr. shrugged his shoulders at the notion of his son being a doctor versus a professional football player. "Uh, it is nice if that is what he wants. I don't see how it expresses his love for football, though?"

"You know what, I can't deal with you right now." She told him.

Later in the evening, the family sat down for dinner. It did not take long for Michael Sr. to joke about his son's career choice. "So Junior, I mean son," he corrected himself when he saw his wife's facial expression. "Your momma said you want to be a foot doctor, is that right?"

Proud of his future career, Michael II corrected his father. "Dad, I am not going to be a foot doctor. You know, I will be a sports doctor like Dr. Brown."

"Oh, okay, you want to be around players but not play the game. I guess that is all right too." Mr. Grayeson told his son.

Larry quickly offered his desire to be a professional football player, so he's not outdone. Since learning about his mother's return, Larry became more determined to maintain Mr. Grayeson's attention. He knows football meant more to the older gentlemen than anything else.

"Clink," the fork forcefully hit the plate as Laverne became frustrated with Larry's interrupting her son's communication with his father. "I am sure, Larry, that you will be successful with whatever you choose. Now Michael, why don't you explain to your father why you chose to be an Orthopedic doctor?" Michael II, with pride, explained to his father how he intended to impact the sports community with his study. Larry ate in silence as he listened to his foster brother's dreams. He felt reassured because his foster father looked at him several times and nodded.

8 DON'T YOU JUDGE ME

Sidney stared at the calendar and focused on two important dates she circled, October 14 and October 16. It weighed heavily on her that the court date was two days before her son's birthday. She prayed to have him home by then, and her lawyer, Richard, was aware of her desire.

While Sidney was praying and hoping, her son was busy planning his birthday party with Michael. Since the two boys wanted to party at the roller-skating rink, Laverne hired a local planner to work out the details. The party was a great distraction for the family, who was also worried about the court case on the 14th.

A week before the hearing, Michael Sr. stood at the large bay window looking at the children playing. His heart sunk at the thought of his family dynamics changing within days. It isn't easy to keep his emotions away from his wife and children, so he chooses to work longer hours.

Laverne had her hands full with the party while trying to keep the happy family appearance around friends. She had mixed feelings about the impending judgment ruling and her son's future.

Michael II and Larry were oblivious to the troubling hearts of the adults. Their excitement about the birthday party carried over to their nightly dinner on the Saturday before the court visit. Michael Sr., happy to talk about anything to refocus his mind, joined in the conversation about roller skating.

The laughter around the table was welcoming to the parents. At the night's end, Laverne felt disoriented with all the pretending. Finally, lying in bed, she exhaled. Hearing her sigh, her husband asked, "what do you think will happen?"

"At this point, I don't know, but I am so over it now. I only want us to return to normal and stop pretending everything is good. Are you okay if Larry goes back to his mother?" She asked.

"To be honest, I am not sure. We have put so much into this boy that it would be shameful for him to leave now. Plus, there's still so much more we could teach him." He responded.

As they drifted off to sleep, the couple had no clear sense of what the future had in store for them. Although the Grayeson slept calmly, Sidney tossed and turned in her bed because having Larry back home with her was the main thing keeping her sanity. Staring at the ceiling, she eventually dozed off to sleep.

The weeks leading up to the court case were nerve-racking for both families, and now it was time for Michael Sr. to meet Larry's mother. Arriving early at the courthouse, Sidney waited patiently for Richard. Every couple that passed by her, she wondered if they had her son. Twenty minutes before their case, Richard hurried into the court corridor. He had previously prepped the eager mother of the possible questions from the opposing lawyer and the Judge but felt the need to review them again.

Walking into the courtroom, a wave of dread came over Sidney. She sat behind the long table with two chairs on the right side of the room. Sitting on the left side were Laverne and Michael Grayeson, along with their lawyer George Bronston. It was the first time the ladies saw each other.

Observing the woman across the room, she was not what Laverne had envisioned. This woman looked beautiful and hopeful, but the purpose of the case was not about how she looked.

After everyone entered, the door in the front of the courtroom opened, and the bailiff walked in and yelled, "all rise, the honorable Judge Canister is entering the room." Judge Canister entered and sat on the bench. "You may be seated," he spoke before looking around the room.

The clerk handed him the folder and informed him about the case, "Plaintiff, in this case, is asking for you to overturn the guardianship previously granted by the court. She wants her son back."

The Judge looked at the defendants and then at the Plaintiff. His eyes met with a shocked Sidney's. Although she was older, he would recognize her anywhere. Seeing the face from the past surprised Larry's mother.

The women at Exceptional Personal Services never knew their companions' real names or occupations unless they shared. Sidney always thought the man sitting in front of her surname was Mr. Martin. Amelia did not explain her departure to the other ladies or her clients when she became pregnant. She never made the connection when Richard told her the Judge's name.

Judge Canister tried to keep his composure. He instructed Richard to present his case after getting confirmation both parties were ready. He could not stop staring at Sidney. Because Richard was speaking, he had a good excuse to look in that direction. His mind kept wandering back to the last time he saw her. He zoned out until he heard 'son' and 'Larry Martin.' Curious, the Judge asked more questions about her son, including his age. Sidney's lawyer offered to call her to testify, but the Judge did not find it warranted. At that point, Richard rested his side of the case.

George Bronston was aware of the Judge's displeasure with degrading women or using their career choices as leverage in a case. He decided to use her hospitalization and diagnosis to outline why Larry should remain with the Grayeson family. The Judge asked several questions about the reason for her hospitalization, and Sidney stood up before dutifully answering all the questions while staring at the Judge.

Laverne's lawyer noticed the expression on the Judge's face and immediately expressed his client's concern for Larry's safety. He also asked the Judge to give them permanent custody of the boy.

Sidney grabbed Richard's arm at that suggestion. Judge Canister listened to both parties but wanted to wait before ruling on the case. Seizing the opportunity, Richard asks the Judge to grant Sidney visitation rights to spend Larry's birthday with him. Looking at the pain in Sidney's eyes, he briefly remembered her joy. He felt compelled to agree with the request. He ordered the Grayeson to arrange visitation with the young man's mother.

It was at the Judge's discretion to call witnesses or prolong the hearing, but Judge Canister did neither. Martin copied Sidney's address on paper before handing the folder back to the clerk. "All Rise," the bailiff called out, then the Judge left the room.

Sidney rose on her weak feet and watched the man from her past walk away. There was not enough time to collect herself when Laverne approached. "Hello, I am Laverne Grayeson, and this is my husband, Michael." She introduced herself.

The distracted mother forced herself to exchange the handshake with the family. "I am Sidney. How is my Larry doing?" She asked.

Hearing her refer to Larry as her own was another dagger in Michael's heart. Recognizing the change in his breathing, Laverne quickly answered, "he is fine. My son Michael and Larry share the same birthday, so their party will be at the skating rink. You are welcome to come by."

"I would love to spend his birthday with him. Thanks for the invitation. Does he talk about me much?" Sidney asked.

"Not really," Michael answered callously.

"My husband meant that Larry's been busy with sports and school. Having another boy of his age in the house has distracted him. I know he misses you." Laverne chimed in quickly.

A sudden awkwardness fell in the room. Exiting the courtroom and courthouse, Sidney was excited about seeing her son and confused about seeing Martin on the bench. She was not the only one thinking about the encounter. Judge Canister entered his chamber, closed the door, and pulled the pillow from the chair to muffle his scream. His emotions consisted of both joy and anger.

9 IT'S PARTY TIME

"Happy Birthday!" family and friends shouted as the two teenagers beamed happily. All the planning cumulated into this evening's events. Sidney chose a blue floral long-sleeved jumpsuit with a fall jacket to meet her son. Walking into the skating rink, she looked around to find her son. Spotting him in the corner surprised her because he had drastically changed from the skinny little boy to a taller and stockier young man. "Will he remember me?" She thought to herself.

As she got closer to the group, Larry saw her and ran over, "mommy, mommy," he called out, then hugged her tight with happiness.

Hello, my baby. You have grown so much." Sidney, with tears in her eyes, hugged and kissed her son. "I missed you so much." She told him.

"I missed you too, mommy. Come meet my brother." Larry replied as he grabbed hold of her hand.

Sidney waited more than two years to see her baby's face, and now she is listening to him calling a stranger his family. Her heart ached, but she put on a brave face as she followed her excited son. "Michael, Michael, my mother is here. Mommy, this is my brother Michael." He spoke aloud.

"Hello, Michael. It is nice to meet you." Larry's mother told him, holding back the tears.

"It's nice to meet you, ma'am," Michael responded before joining the kids on the rink.

Standing at the table, she watched the teenagers skating from the rink to the table to grab snacks. Laverne, who had spotted the woman earlier, made her way to greet her. "Sidney, it is so good of you to join us. Come and sit with us. The non-skaters, including me, are hiding from their kids."

"Hi Laverne, yes, it's great to be here. You did a lovely job." Sidney answered, trying to hide her pain.

Following the older woman, she walked a short distance and met the parents of her son's friends. Everyone seemed welcoming and charming except for Michael Sr., who was busy skating with the kids as a chaperone. Entering the adult space and seeing Sidney, his facial expression changed.

Although he greeted her, his tone was less than friendly. His wife gave him a stern look to say be nice. Michael Sr. turned his attention to the other parents trying to enlist them in going onto the skating rink. Seconds later, Larry skated past Michael to his mother before any of them could answer. "Mommy, come skate with us." He commanded.

"It's been a long time since I've been on the skates, plus I am more comfortable on rollerblades because it's just like ice skates." She told her son.

"I am sure they have rollerblades as well." Laverne chimed in.

"If they do, then I would love to join you." The young man's mother told him.

"Let's go see if they have them." Larry pulled on his mother.

Nudge by his wife, Michael Sr., reluctantly took Sidney to the front and inquired about rollerblades. Secretly he hoped none was available to prohibit her from having fun with his son. To his disappointment, they had some rollerblades for the brave few.

Finding her size, the gentleman behind the counter handed them to her. Within minutes, Sidney was on the floor skating with the children. She moved so gently and free-flowing that all the kids, including Michael II, soon joined her. Even though they were on skates, she was able to teach them some roller moves that made it more fun.

Michael Sr. left the skating floor and joined his wife, who saw the fury in his eyes. Quickly, she whispered in his ear to remind him that the woman was Larry's mother. Trying not to show his displeasure in front of the other parents, Michael Sr. pushed a smile to his face.

Martin Canister tracked Sidney after seeing her in the courtroom. Through his sources, he got the location of the party.

Curious to see what her son looked like; he unconsciously drove to the skating rink. Once inside, he could not help noticing Sidney skating. It reminded him of the days they used to go ice skating on his business trips to Utah. Her gentleness still causes his heart to beat fast.

Sliding into the corner, he tried to work out which of the two teenagers with her was Larry, and it did not take long for him to figure it out. Satisfied with what he saw, he slipped out of the building before anyone saw him. While sitting in his car, he made a note to have his clerk schedule a meeting with both lawyers.

The end of the party saddens Sidney because she must leave without her son. As Larry walked her to the car, he asked, "mommy am I going to see you again?" The sadness in his voice touched his mother's heart and Laverne's.

Cupping his face with her hands, Sidney answered honestly, looking at him and then Laverne. "I am doing my best to see you more often. I am working out the visitation timing with Mr. and Mrs. Grayeson. You would be coming home with me if I had my way. I will see you soon. I love you so much."

Michael Sr. stood by the door, watching the interaction between mother and son.

Although Sidney was leaving Larry behind, the foster father was not impressed with the attention she was giving her son. He thought the mother establishing a bond meant his hold on Larry would diminish. Instinctively he called out, "Hey, son," to get Larry's attention. "We are getting ready to go; say goodbye now."

His words angered Sidney but leaving her son with a smile was important. Kissing him on the cheek, she waited by her car and watched him run over to the foster family. Leaning against the car as Michael drove off, she pulled out some change from her purse, walked to the payphone on the side of the rink, and called Richard to schedule another visit as soon as possible. As she was about to climb into her vehicle, she looked at the car across the parking lot. "Is that Martin?" She questioned herself.

10 A HARD DECISION

Adhering to the Judge's request, Richard Pickerton and George Bronston met in his chamber to discuss Larry. The Judge ordered, during their conversation, an informal meeting with the young man to get his opinion. George delivered the request immediately after leaving the Judge's chamber.

Michael Sr. entered the information on the calendar hanging in the hallway and circled the date in red.

On the day of the meeting, Michael Sr., Laverne, and Larry arrived at the courthouse nervous about the possible decision from one conversation. Laverne attempted to walk her foster son into the Judge's chamber, but the clerk would not allow her. Pointing to the chair, the clerk instructed Larry to sit and wait for the Judge to arrive, then closed the door behind her.

The dialogue between Larry and Judge Canister did not last long because no one knew he had ulterior motives. The Judge asked poignant questions about Larry's mother, foster parents, and school as part of the ruse. Before the meeting ended, a woman in a white lab coat entered the chamber.

The bright young man instantly questioned the purpose of the doctor's visit. The Judge informed him the test was to confirm that Sidney was his mother, and Larry had no reason to believe otherwise. Seconds after the technician swabbed his mouth, Judge Canister's clerk escorted him to Laverne and Michael. The clerk sternly instructed him not to discuss the conversation under any circumstances as they listened. Her tone scared all three of them. A week later, Martin received the result of the paternity test. Putting the envelope in his desk drawer, he notified both lawyers he was ready to give his ruling. The lawyers promptly contacted their clients with the court date. Because it was on a school day, Laverne sent the children to school instead.

The day started with an overrun of nerves in both homes. Sidney sat on the side of her bed for a few minutes realizing how important the Judge's decision would be to her future. Finally, dressed in a light-yellow stripe dress with a white jacket, she checked her light makeup before walking out of the house.

Laverne and Michael took a few minutes before getting dressed to settle their nerves. Laverne wore a white jumpsuit and a yellow jacket, while Michael wore blue denim jeans and a white shirt. Checking her hair and makeup in the hall mirror, the proud mother walked out to the car. Prep complete, both families were on their way to the courthouse.

Parking in the lower lot, Sidney began to hyperventilate. "Stop it, just breathe." She scolded herself. Feeling better, she got out of the car and walked into the building. While she was entering, Michael Grayeson parked the vehicle in the upper lot. His hands began to shake uncontrollably soon after taking them off the steering wheel. Laverne placed her left hand on his right arm and whispered, "it will be

okay no matter the decision; just breathe." Smiling at his wife, he tried to remain calm. The couple walked together, holding hands as they entered the courthouse.

Once again, Sidney is facing the family caring for her son. They exchanged pleasantries before entering the courtroom. Within minutes the bailiff was calling out for them to rise. Larry's mother began to sweat under her arms and down her back. Martin told them to sit down, trying not to look directly at Sidney. He began, "Cases involving children are often difficult to give a ruling because as Judges, every decision we make can have consequences and, in this case, a boy's welfare could be compromised. Miss Washington, you want this court to vacate a previous decision, so your son could return home. Mr. and Mrs. Grayeson, you want the child to remain with you and gain full custody. All parties have shown great love towards the boy, and both sides presented compelling arguments to justify their requests. However, it is up to me to make the right decision based on the evidence and my conversation with the young man you all call Larry."

Hearing that he spoke to her son was a surprise to Sidney. She whispered to Richard, "When did he speak to my baby?"

Richard patted her hand to refocus on the Judge, who was still talking, "I must consider his wishes and what I felt would give him the best path for continuous growth. Since he expressed his desire to be with his mother and the Grayeson, Larry will return to his mother at the end of the school year. Ms. Washington will maintain visitation until then." As soon as the judge announced his decision, Michael Sr. jumped up and yelled out, "that is not fair. He has been with us all this time," before George could stop him.

The Judge looked sternly at the heartbroken man and spoke, "Sit down, Mr. Grayeson. Another outburst like that, and I will remove you from my courtroom. As I was saying, Larry is to remain with his foster family until the last day of his school year. That is my final decision. You are adults, so work out the transition after that date. Any questions?" He stood up, looked around, and walked out of the courtroom.

Sidney squealed in excitement after learning her son will return home. Understanding how disappointed the other family was, she tried to hold back her enthusiasm. She walks over to the family and initiates the dialogue, "Thank you for taking such loving care of my son. He told me he has a game on Saturday, but I would like to pick him up Friday evening and bring him back Sunday. I will also make sure he is on time for the game." She told Laverne.

"It was a pleasure taking care of Larry. I do not see a problem with him spending the weekend with you. What do you think, honey?" She asked her husband.

"This decision is ridiculous. I will meet you outside." He responded and then stormed out of the courtroom.

Apologizing for her husband's behavior, Laverne extended her hand to Sidney. Larry's mother had no warm feelings toward Michael and ignored his childish behavior. Exiting the courthouse, the joy in her heart caused Sidney to dance when she reached her car.

The night before Larry's visit, his mother began arranging his room then her doorbell rang. Surprised by the sound, she hesitantly walked to the door. Looking through the peephole, she saw Martin on the other side. She called out. "What are you doing here?"

"Please let me in. I want to talk to you." He told her.

"Go away, please." She told him.

"I have a few questions. You owe me some answers, and then I will leave." He told her.

Opening the door slowly, Sidney stepped aside so he could enter. Martin walked into the foyer and waited for her to pass by him. She walked quickly into the living room to put some distance between them. "Isn't your being here a conflict of interest?" Her question was to the point.

"Since I already rendered my verdict and the case is closed, it's no longer a conflict." He told her.

"How convenient for you. What are your questions?" She asked sternly.

"Besides the fact that you surprised me when you showed up in my courtroom after disappearing without a word." He startles her.

"Wait, what? First, that is not a question, it's a statement, and second, I never left without notice." She corrected him.

"I waited for hours at the hotel, but you were a no-show. When I contacted Amelia, she said you left without any notice. I call that disappearing, and now you have a child." He told her, trying to sound angry.

"I am not surprised that selfish witch lied. As soon as I told her I was pregnant, she kicked me out and threatened me if I tried to contact you or anyone associated with her, including the other ladies. She left me on my own, pregnant with little money. I tried to find you throughout the years, but how was I supposed to know Martin was not your last name? Anyway, that was a long time ago. Why are you mentioning the past?" She snapped at him in a raised tone.

"Yes, it was a while ago, but it is my opportunity to express my feelings. I have bottled it up long enough." He told her.

Sidney tried to ignore his innuendos about their relationship. Moving to the corner of the room by the marbled fireplace to avoid looking at him, she started shifting the figurines on the mantle.

11 POOR SIDNEY

"Oh my gosh, you are so beautiful. I never thought anyone could get even more gorgeous, but here you are. When you disappeared, I was angry."

"Again, I did not disappear, and it's not a question; plus, you seem to do alright for yourself." She told him cynically with clenched teeth.

"Your leaving, not disappearing, caused me to put all my focus on my career to hide my broken heart. When I received my appointment as a judge specializing in family court, I never thought I would see you there. Seeing you reminded me how much I missed you." He told her, trying to stop himself from moving closer and pulling her into his arms.

"I do not need to hear this right now. You do not know the real meaning of being heartbroken. After court, I did my research and found out you were married. Please stop acting as though I left you alone. You led me to believe you were single when we were together. Our relationship blossomed on a lie, and you expect me to be happy to see you again. It is time for you to go." Sidney motioned to the door.

"Don't you feel anything? We were making plans to get married, remember?" He asked softly.

Turning to face him, "plans, what a joke. How were you going to do that when you were already married? Explain that one to me." The angry woman pointed at him.

"It is true. I was wrong not telling you about my marriage. The plan was to file for divorce before you found out. I know that was stupid, but I went to the hotel to propose the night you disappeared. If you accepted, I was going to tell her it was over. Leaving the hotel, I felt lost. I had not realized how trapped I was until I saw you. Seeing you made me feel alive again. I would give everything up to be with you. I am still in love with you." He confessed to her.

"Stop saying I disappeared because I did not. You cannot come here and tell me you love me. I cannot hear this right now, and it isn't fair. You said what you wanted to say; now leave." Sidney rebuffed him, stepping backward to keep the distance between them.

"Where you ever going to tell me that he is my son?" He asked annoyedly, knowing that talking about Larry would maintain her attention.

"Why are you asking about my son? I do not know if he's yours. I was with other men, remember." She lied, knowing he was the only man she had actual intercourse with during her time at the agency.

"I know you weren't having sex with other men, plus the DNA test confirmed it." He remarked. Sidney was unaware that he pressed Amelia for the truth after her appearance in his courtroom.

"What DNA test are you talking about?" She snapped at him. After a small pause, she asked, "Is that why you tricked my son into speaking to you?"

Slowly walking towards her, he confessed. "Yes, I was curious about him."

"You had no right; you had no right. Get out. GET OUT!" She yelled. Martin's heart broke again hearing her throwing him out of her townhouse.

Feeling dejected, Martin left Sidney's home, vowing to never give up on their union. The following day, a joyful Sidney arrived at the Grayeson to pick up Larry, and after a brief, cordial exchange, it did not take long for her to drive home. She happily showed her son around the townhouse and was especially excited about his football-themed room.

The mother and son spent the evening reminiscing and catching up on missed events. The next day, she took him to the football stadium and sat by some of the parents she met at the party to watch her son play. Later that evening, they ate dinner and watched old family-friendly movies. Although Sidney wanted him to stay home, she brought him back to the Grayeson's late Sunday evening.

Along with summer, the end of the school year arrived, and no one was happier than Sidney. She arranged with the family to get Larry on

Saturday to give them one more evening with him. Sitting in the car, Larry waved goodbye to his other family. Soon as the car reached the end of the subdivision, Sidney turned on the radio so Larry could find a station. They sang all the way home. Even though Larry loved being with the Grayeson, spending time with his mother was better than he had hoped.

Watching his football dreams driving away, Michael Sr. became angry with everyone he encountered. Laverne pulled him aside one afternoon to remind him that his real son needed him just as much, if not more. Forcing himself, the disappointed father began spending more time with his child. One Saturday evening, Michael II, with excitement, showed his father all the scientific and medical information about keeping the players safe he found. Within two months, father and son bonded over sports terminology and techniques. Michael II had not realized how much he missed his father's attention until he got it.

Meanwhile, Larry and Sidney were having great fun going to the beach on short trips, and she even found a football coach to train him during the off-season. As both families settled into a routine, Martin showed up at the house mid-July for a visit. He disguised it as checking on Larry's welfare, but Sidney knew better. "Is something wrong?" The young man asked nervously.

"No, son, I am only here to follow up on your wellbeing," Martin answered.

"What about the test?" He pressed.

Martin had to think about the question for a few minutes, and then it came back to him. "Yes, she passed," was his response, not to prolong the question.

After that, Martin became a regular visitor to Sidney's home. Since Larry visited the Grayeson periodically, Martin and Sidney would often be alone. The grateful mother was still adamant about not dating a married man. However, that did not deter Martin from pursuing her. Years passed, and the beginning of September meant a new school year, and Sidney's son was officially a high school senior.

Arriving home one afternoon, she found a letter from the mortgage company in her mailbox. Her mind flashed back to her eviction experience; however, this notice differed. Reading it quickly, she saw it says zero balance. Puzzled by the number, she instantly contacted the bank. After learning the balance was correct, she suspected Martin had paid it. "Every year, he does something. I cannot seem to get rid of him, urgh." She mouthed aloud.

Sidney, Larry, and the Grayeson's routines were going smoothly. Everyone was happy until November 24, 1984.

Since it was the weekend after Thanksgiving, Sidney and Larry went shopping and then stopped at a restaurant to enjoy dinner. While waiting on the food, Martin appeared at the table. Surprised by his presence, Sidney tried to make the conversation quick. Scanning the room, she saw a lady sitting in the corner watching him intensely. She alerted him of the woman's facial expression, but the obsessed man ignored it. Martin went back to his wife's table after Sidney insisted. She enjoyed her meal and laughed at Larry's silly jokes before leaving the restaurant.

The small family was on top of the world as they crossed the street to go to the car. Sidney looked to her left to see a car speeding towards them. As she pushed her son out of the way, the vehicle hit Sidney tossing her up in the air before landing on the hard street. All the pedestrians were horrified, then a young man began yelling to the nearby shop owner to call for an ambulance.

Seeing his mother on the ground and blood running from her head, Larry started yelling, "Mommy, mommy, get up, please get up." The tears were streaming down his cheeks as an older woman held him back from touching his mother. Within minutes the ambulance was on the scene along with the police. The EMT workers took Sidney and Larry to the hospital while the police officers gathered information.

12 HIDDEN TRUTH

"Oh no, no," Martin kept yelling as he saw his wife's speeding car hit Sidney. Astonished at her action, he ran over to the crowd to ascertain how Sidney was doing without drawing attention to himself. Hearing the siren, he returned to his car and followed them to the hospital.

Meanwhile, Samantha Canister began shaking as she drove home. Expecting to see her husband home a few minutes behind her, she started screaming, throwing an expensive vase and other expensive figurines at the wall in the living room when he did not turn up. "You bastard, you bastard." She cried aloud.

Back at the hospital, Martin was able to talk his way into the back area of the emergency room. Larry saw him walking through the door and ran towards him. "They won't tell me about my mommy." He yelled out. Martin hugged him to comfort him during his distress. It was the first time the Judge embraced his son.

The young man was as tall as him but physically larger. Feeling helpless, he searched for a doctor who could provide answers. Using his judicial status, the older man found a nurse, and after a brief conversation, she called Dr. Ketchered, the doctor responsible for Sidney. Martin asked, "can you tell us about Sidney Washington's condition as the man approached them? She was the car accident victim that came here in the ambulance about thirty minutes ago." He asked.

"Who are you to the patient?" Dr. Ketchered spouted.

Martin was not going to disclose the truth about his relationship with Sidney, nor was he about to reveal he was Larry's father, so he chose the simple answer. "I am a close friend, but this is her son, Larry."

Looking at Larry, the doctor asked, "young man, are you okay with me sharing information about your mother in front of this man?"

The young boy only wanted to know about his mother, so he nodded yes to the doctor. "Okay then, Ms. Washington suffered a massive head injury, broken collar bone, pelvic bone, and a broken jaw. To help with her healing, we have placed her in an induced coma. Honestly, she has a long road to recovery ahead of her." The doctor told them both as he looked at Larry.

Everything the doctor said sounded horrific to both men standing in front of the doctor. Larry turned his attention to Martin. "What does that mean?" He inquired through the tears. The stocky footballer appeared as a small child before his biological father.

"It means your mother won't be coming home for a while." The older man answered.

"What am I supposed to do now? Am I allowed to stay home by myself?" He whispered in between his constant crying.

"Do not worry, son. I will arrange something." Martin tried to console him.

At the Grayeson home, Laverne was busy with her clients. She typically does not see patients on the holiday weekend but made an exception on that day. A few minutes after Laverne's last client left her home office, she stretched and walked into the kitchen to make a snack. Watching the clock, she tried to determine the dinner menu for herself. Sitting down to eat her tuna with lettuce sandwich, she graced her food and turned on the television.

Moments after it came on, the news station broke through the program "Breaking News: This afternoon, a hit and run accident left a mother in a coma. Witnesses said the mother and son were crossing the road when a car sped up towards them. Another witness recounted how the mother pushed her son out of the way." The news station did not release a picture of Sidney or Larry. As she listened, Laverne felt sad for the family, but it never crossed her mind that the mother and son were Sidney and Larry.

It did not take long after Martin made several calls to obtain the Grayeson's phone number and permission to call them. "Ring, ring," the home phone that hung on the wall separating the living room and kitchen began ringing. Taking the final bite of her sandwich, Laverne walked over to answer her phone. "Hello." She spoke, trying to swallow at the same time.

"Hello, is this Mrs. Grayeson?" The male voice on the other end asked.

"Yes, it is. How can I help you?" She replied.

"This is Judge Canister. I am at the hospital with Larry, the young man once in your care. His mother was in an accident earlier, so would you be able to resume temporary custody of him until his mother regains the ability to care for him?" He asked.

"Sorry, are you saying the accident I just saw on the news involved my Larry? Oh my gosh, oh my gosh. Yes, we will care for him. Where is he now? I must get to him?" She spoke with haste and concern. Obtaining the hospital's name, she hung up from Judge Canister and paged her husband.

Michael Sr. was at a medical symposium with his son learning about new techniques coaches and doctors may use to keep the players safe. To his surprise, the older man was intrigued by the various available tools. He was looking at the body pads when his pager buzzed. Looking at the number, he stepped out to call his wife. Laverne carefully relayed the message from Judge Canister to her husband. She insisted he finish the visit with their son, and she will get Larry. Her husband hearing about the accident was sad for what Larry had witnessed. Part of him was happy he was coming home, but the other was disappointed in how it happened. Agreeing with his wife, he returned to the program, and she rushed to the hospital.

Reuniting Laverne with Larry, Martin left the hospital. The hardest part of his day was about to begin. He must decide if he would report his wife as the offender or allow her to get away with it. As he drove up to his house, it was evident that someone had already decided for him. Martin watched the officer escort his wife in handcuffs out of the house as he pulled up. Parking next to the police car, he tried to get her attention, but Samantha looked directly in front of her. Martin called his lawyer and followed the patrol car to the police station with his mind racing.

13 A HEART ISSUE

Laverne Grayeson was conflicted about allowing Larry to see his mother in her comatose state. Eventually, she gave in after seeing Larry's painful expression. Minutes after getting the attention of the ICU nurse, who escorted the patient's son into the hospital room, Laverne waited by the nurse's station.

Walking into the room, the heartbroken boy looked at his mother for a few minutes, still in disbelief. He sat by his mother's bedside, held her hand, and began praying, "Lord, please heal my mother. Mommy, I love you so much. Please do not leave me again. I don't want to grow up without you." As the tears rolled down his face, he held her hand to his cheek, kissed it, then laid it back next to her. Ten minutes later, he kissed her forehead and then left the room.

Back with Laverne, he hugged her and whispered, "thank you." His expression of gratitude broke her heart. Fighting the tears, she embraced the young man before taking him to his home to gather his things.

Meanwhile, Michael Sr. tried to stay engaged in his son's program. The original plan was to join the presenters for dinner at the end of the presentation, but the boy's father changed his mind. After the organizer's speech, Michael II, excited about the dinner, walked over to his father with the restaurant's information. His father's facial expression suddenly quenched his excitement. "What's wrong, dad?" He asked.

"We must go home now. Sorry, I know you were looking forward to the dinner, but next time."

Saddened by the last-minute change, the young man followed his father to the car. The two hours car ride seemed like five hours with the deafening silence. Unfortunately, young Michael did not know the situation with Larry's mother.

Pulling into the garage, both men exited and made their way into the house. Turning the corner into the living room, Michael II was surprised to see Larry sitting at the kitchen island and his mother standing on the other side with a sad look. Michael Sr. rushed over, scooped the boy into his arms, and hugged him tightly. "I am so sorry about your mom. How are you doing?" He asked in a sincere tone.

As Larry opened his mouth to speak, Michael II asked, "what's going on?" All three people looked at him, realizing he did not know what had happened earlier. Concerned for her son, Laverne walked over to him and explained the accident.

Feeling bad about the woman's situation, Michael also consoled Larry. He hoped he would not lose his father's attention now that Larry had returned.

As the days passed, Martin's visits to the hospital became daily. He still hoped for her to recover and come back to him fully. Although he attended the hearing and sentencing, he resigned from his wife's crime.

On his only visit to the prison, he wanted to know why she did it. Samantha's eyes looked empty, sitting across from the man she allowed to consume her life. "How are you doing in here?" He asked, trying to sound concerned.

"How do you think I am doing in a 2x4 cell." She responded in a cold tone.

"Sorry. You know there is nothing I could have done, right? I cannot understand what happened. Why did you do it? Those people did nothing to you. That woman is lying in the hospital in a coma. Was it worth spending six years of your life in a cell?" He asked, trying to get an emotional reaction from her.

His wife spoke in a monotone, emotionless voice, looking in a daze. "For years, I had to compete with that woman for your affections. Do you think I did not know about your secret hotel rendezvous, trips, and late-night phone conversations when you would go to the bathroom? When you stopped seeing her, I thought; finally, I got my husband back, but I did not.

Your body was there but not your heart. I knew something changed when you came home excited. You had the same look in your eyes as when you were with her back then. I started following you when the mysterious late evenings and weekend meetings began again. Everything seemed normal until you went to the skating rink. I thought, "he was having a midlife crisis," but who was I kidding? I was about to leave, but I noticed you stayed in your car after leaving the building and kept looking at the entrance door.

It did not take long for me to face reality because your lover came walking out the door. I got curious after seeing her with a boy; I presume he is her son. I tried talking to you about it that night and the next day, and it bothered me that you were never available for me.

I had enough, so Monday, I went to your office to force you to have the conversation, but you were in the middle of a hearing. Yes, I talked Jessica into allowing me to wait in your office. I cannot explain why, but something made me open the draw, and there it was." She stopped.

Martin did not need her to tell him what she saw because he already knew he hid the paternity test there. "You found the test result." He spoke in a cowardly voice.

Leaning over the table, she spoke through her teeth, "yes, I found the freaking test showing you had a son. Throughout our marriage, I wanted children, but you insisted you never wanted any, so what was I supposed to do with that information? If that was not enough, you kept going over her house, paying her mortgage, then setting up a college fund for him. I could have ignored all of that until you publicly humiliated me by trying to show your affection for them at dinner. It was as though you could not help yourself. I reached my breaking point. I thought if I could make them go away, life would be back to normal. I got that wrong, didn't I? You could not even drive home to see about me after it happened. No, you went to the hospital instead. Prison helped me realize she was not the problem; it was you.

My only regret is that you were not in front of the car." Samantha leaned back in her chair and smiled for the first time since she sat down. Her smile looked wicked and scared Martin.

He did not get a chance to respond because the guard announced visitation was over. Walking out of the woman's prison, he looked back, shook his head, and left. Judge Martin Canister never visited his wife at the jail again. Although he tried to understand her action, he could not forgive her for trying to take his love away from him. He asked his lawyer to draw up the divorce papers a few weeks later. Samantha, agreeing with the terms, signed the documents without contention. Not long after her sentencing, she drafted a book detailing all the sorted details of his affair and the breakdown that led to the accident. She tried to publish it, but when word got to the Judge, he made it impossible for any publishing company to publish her work. Samantha released it as a blog instead.

Michael Sr. and Laverne took turns bringing Larry to the hospital to visit his mother every Sunday afternoon or after his football games. Michael II felt the change in his father's attention. Slipping back into the shadows, he resented his house guest and father. Young Michael became more determined to focus on his studies.

One afternoon as his parents were visiting the hospital, he decided to clean out his old chest and found the number for Dr. Thelia Brown. Instinctively, he went to the phone and dialed her number without fully thinking it through.

14 WHAT ABOUT ME?

Ring, ring, the phone rang four times before Dr. Brown answered. Young Michael was about to place the handset down when he heard the voice. "Hello, hello."

Uncertain of his reason for calling, he responded, "good afternoon, Dr. Brown," assuming it was her on the other end of the phone.

"Good afternoon; who's calling?" The voice on the other end replied.

"This is Michael Grayeson. I met you at football practice several years ago. I am not sure if you remember me." He spoke nervously on the phone.

"Oh yes. You are the young man who was fascinated with sports and medicine. How are you doing?" She asked.

Thrilled that she remembered him, Michael felt more comfortable speaking to her. "I am doing well. I am about to graduate from high school, and you mentioned helping me choose the right college. Are you able to still help me? If you cannot, it's okay too." He told her.

"Is it that time already? I would love to discuss your future and help you with the right school. How about lunch next Saturday?" She asked him.

"Lunch sounds great. I only have my learner's permit, so I will see if my mom can take me." He answered with excitement.

Michael II knew his father's chances of taking him to meet Dr. Brown were slim to none with Larry's return. The call ended after both agreed on a restaurant to meet. The short conversation with Dr. Brown brought joy to the young man. He went to the kitchen to find food after he finished cleaning. Shortly after making a grill cheese sandwich Michael II sat at the kitchen island by himself.

Although he still had a little joy from the conversation, he could not help feeling alone. Before the accident, he knew he had his mother's support no matter what. Now both parents are more concerned about Larry than him. Unexpectedly, tears welled up in his eyes. Solemnly he ate his sandwich while staring at the wall. Finishing the grilled cheese, he walked to the living room and stared through the window before retreating to the basement.

Laverne and Michael Sr. sat in the waiting area and waited for Larry to visit his mother. It did not take long for her to notice Judge Martin walking through the door. He was standing by the receptionist's desk when Larry exited the elevator. The young man smiled when he left his mother's room, so he overlooked the judge. Laverne rose from the chair and met him halfway. "You are looking happier than when you went upstairs." She remarked.

"I just spoke to the doctor. He said that the swelling on my mom's brain had gone down. They are keeping her in a coma, but he said it is good news. Oh, he also said her bones are healing nicely." Sidney's son told his caregiver.

"That is wonderful news. Michael, did you hear that?" She responded.

Michael Sr. did not want to show his disapproval of Larry's enthusiasm about his mother. He replied, "yes, but she still has a long way to go before getting better. Let's go home." Stretching his hand towards the door, the older gentleman escorted them out of the building.

Driving home, Larry asked Michael Sr. about taking him to the football tryouts scheduled in a week. The foster father proudly agreed to take the young man to college. Sadly, he forgot that he promised to attend his son's senior final project presentation the same day as the tryout. Young Michael had been working secretly on his project for several months as a surprise for his father.

Entering the house, Laverne called out to Michael, so he knew they were home. He ran up the stairs to greet them and find out about Sidney's recovery. "How's your mother doing?" He asked Larry.

"The doctor said the swelling has gone down on her brain, and her broken bones are healing." He happily reported to his foster brother.

The boys embraced and then sat at the kitchen island. Larry told young Michael his dad would take him to the football college tryouts without thinking. Michael II realizing the tryout was on the same day as his presentation, shouted, "Dad, you promised you were going to attend my program."

Michael Sr. knew he was now in a difficult position. Looking at both boys, he explained how important it would be for Larry to get a football scholarship. His son immediately felt betrayed that he chose Larry over him. "What about me? When am I going to be important to you?" The young man asked in a disappointed tone.

"I am sorry. I did not know you had something on the same day." Larry tried to apologize.

"It does not matter because he should have remembered. The only thing that matters to him is you and your football, and I hate you both." He yelled and stormed off to his room.

Laverne, heartbroken for her son, looked angrily at her husband. "You better fix this." She told him and walked away.

Still sitting at the kitchen island, Larry looked at Michael Sr. for help. "Don't worry about it, son. I am sure he will realize how important this is and come around." The older Michael told him as he pulled a beer from the fridge and sat in the living room. Suddenly the house had an eerie feeling.

15 NO REGRETS

The gentle breeze and the birds chirping announced the coldness of winter was leaving, and spring was approaching. Michael II woke up early Saturday morning anxious about his lunch with Dr. Brown. Sitting in his bedroom, he flipped through the many brochures he had collected from school. "One of you will be my home for four years," he mumbled with excitement and fear. He thought he would be making the journey alone because his father had made his choice.

The teenager finally emerged from his room and entered the kitchen. After pulling the bowl from the cabinet and the milk from the fridge, he took his favorite cereal out of the pantry and sat at the kitchen island. He sat alone for ten minutes before Larry joined him in the room. "Morning." The youth told Michael while reaching for the cereal bowl.

"Morning," Michael mumbled as he pushed the box and milk towards Larry.

Both boys sat at the kitchen island and ate in silence. Larry desperately wanted to get back his relationship with his foster brother, but he could not find the right words to say. Finally, in between chews, he spoke. "Do you hate me for coming back?"

The question jarred Michael out of his deep thoughts. "I do not hate you for coming back. I hate my dad for picking you over me again." The response was not what Larry expected. He stared into the bowl of cereal and wished he could erase the last five months.

"Sorry." He mumbled, then immediately put a spoonful of cereal in his mouth. Michael nodded, then got up from the kitchen island and went to the basement.

Watching him leave without a response made Larry miss his mother deeply. Larry returned to his room and stared at the ceiling while lying on the bed. Standing in the hallway, Laverne heard the brief exchange between the boys. Her heart broke even more for them both. She slipped into the hall bathroom, so Michael would not see her. After hearing the basement door open, she went back to her room.

"You have to fix your broken relationship with your son." She told her husband as she stood by the bed.

"There is nothing to fix. Junior is too emotional about the whole thing. He must understand how important it is for Larry to get the football scholarship. He has money from his grandfather for college, but Larry does not have anything saved. He must stop being selfish." Michael Sr. told his wife.

"Do you hear yourself? You are going to regret this. Your son may never forgive you. When Larry returns home, what are you going to do then? You keep forgetting he has a mother, and she will make a full recovery, which means home visits from school will be to her house. All the accolades and notoriety you are trying to get will go to her. In the meantime, your boy feels cast out and rejected by you because he does not want to put on a football outfit. Michael Grayeson, I have never been more ashamed of you than now." She responded before going into the bathroom.

Michael Sr. dismissed his wife's remark, rolled over, and went back to sleep. Laverne walked out of her bedroom shaking her head. She called out to her son for him to get ready. After making herself a cup of coffee, Laverne gently knocked on Larry's door. The concerned guardian asked if she could enter in a soft voice. After giving her permission, Larry sat on the bed, waiting for her to enter the room.

Walking into the bedroom, Laverne saw the sadness in the young man's eyes. "So sorry you are not feeling connected with Michael now. I want you to know it is not your fault. My husband is blind when it comes to certain things. You are very much welcome here, so don't ever question that. I will give it another couple of days, and you both will be remarkably close again." She patted Larry on the arm as she spoke.

"Okay. Can I come with you today?" He asked, seeing his foster mother dressed for the outdoors.

"On this occasion, I will have to say no. Michael has planned a luncheon, and I am dropping him off. Due to his current state of mind, it might be better to do something later. How about all of us go bowling? Would you like that?" Laverne asked.

"Bowling sounds like fun. Okay, I hope Michael will have fun too." He told her.

"I am sure he will," Laverne told him as she winked and left the room.

She placed her coffee mug into the sink and grabbed her purse. "Michael, I am in the car. You would not want to be late, right?" She called her son.

Michael II grabbed his jacket and, with brochures in hand, met his mother in the car. Walking to the vehicle, he dreaded seeing Larry already seated in the passenger side of the vehicle, but it was empty. Buckling his seatbelt, the young man felt a sense of relief. It had been a long time since he spent alone with his mother. "I brought the brochures to share them with Dr. Brown." He spoke aloud.

"That is a great idea. I wonder which one the doctor will recommend." His mother responded.

"Me too. What if Dr. Brown recommends an expensive school? How will I pay for it?" He asked.

"Do not worry about that. Your granddad has taken care of your college fund." The mother proudly informed her son.

"How come I never met granddad or grandma?" He asked.

"Because they both passed away before you were born. After losing my mom to breast cancer, my dad passed from a heart attack three years later. I wish you could have met them, and I know they would have spoiled you rotten." She smiled to keep the tears from whelping up in her eyes.

It did not take long for the mother and son to arrive at the restaurant in the city. Parking in the parking lot, she exited the car and walked a short distance to Maximo's Italian Eatery. Entering the building, she saw Dr. Brown waiting by the reception area. They exchanged pleasantries and sat at the table near the window.

An excited Michael handed Dr. Brown the brochures he had brought with him. Enjoying his enthusiasm, she browsed through the stack quickly and set them on the table.

The doctor was about to speak when the server walked up to the table. "Hello, welcome to Maximo. My name is Natalie, and I'll be your server today. Are you ready to order?" The three patrons look at each other and then at the server. "Can you give us five to ten minutes?" Dr. Brown asked her.

"Yes, sure," Natalie answered, then walked to another table.

The server returned fifteen minutes later to take the drink and food order. All three dove into a conversation about the appropriate college for the young man's career path.

Before Dr. Brown discussed her recommendations, she wanted to determine whether Michael II wanted to be a sports medicine physician or an orthopedic specialist.

Michael II had not realized the difference, so he pressed her to tell him more. Amid her explanation, the food arrived. Michael was intrigued by the depth of information Dr. Brown provided, and food was secondary in his mindset. Gripping onto every word, he decided on both. He would start with Sports Medicine and eventually move into Orthopedic practice.

With the decision made, Dr. Brown offered the University of Virginia, her alma mater, first and then the University of Southern California, which happens to be her husband's alma mater. "Both schools are top-rated," she told him. Calculating the distance of the school from his home in New Jersey, he requested additional schools.

"My son is determined to get the best education, but he is incredibly wise in figuring out what's best for him. The schools you mentioned may be top of the list, but one is extremely far, and the other is too close." Laverne told Dr. Brown with a smile.

"Well, I can certainly understand his position, but those two are it if you want the best education. Lower in my choice would be Michigan University or Ohio State College of Medicine. There are many other schools in other states, such as North Carolina and Florida. I am sure you get the picture. The bottom line is the value you place on your education." She told the mother and son.

Michael Grayeson absorbed a lot of information in the brief time he sat with Dr. Brown. Finally, he asked, "if they require sponsorship, would you sponsor me?" His voice came across as timid, and Dr. Brown immediately corrected him.

"Do you want the sponsorship?" She asked in a stern voice.

"Yes." He answered with a puzzling look on his face.

"Then you need to own the question. As you leave your parents' home, you must be assertive, or the streets will eat you alive within the first couple of months of you being on your own." She told him.

After making him ask several times again in a tone she felt acceptable, she agreed. Dr. Brown also offered to mentor the young man, who quickly accepted.

After just a few minutes with Dr. Brown, young Grayeson felt confident in his ability to make decisions. Since she had another appointment, the doctor left the family at the table. Laverne tried to use the time to have a heart-to-heart with her son. Concerned about his current disposition, Laverne attempted to explain his father's actions. Even though she knew it was no consolation, using Larry's need for a scholarship was her best option. Michael II tried to understand the point of view his mother presented, but it did not stop him from feeling second best to Larry. He felt as though his father pushed him into the shadows of a substitute son. "Mom, I know what you are trying to do, but it does not excuse your husband's actions." He told her.

Laverne knew it was serious when her son did not acknowledge Michael Sr. as his father. Tabling the discussion for another time, they left the restaurant.

Later that day, as promised, the family went bowling, and young Michael did his best to have fun. Although Laverne purposely partnered with Larry so the father and son would be on the same team, it did not work out as expected. Unfortunately, the older Michael did not see how assisting Larry throughout the games infuriated his son.

He mumbled, "I can't wait to leave this stupid place," rolling the ball down the lane. Seconds later, he bowled a strike. His mother was waiting on Larry to finish bowling when he slumped down on the orange seat and whispered, "I am choosing California. I know you'll miss me at least, but I have to go."

Tears filled Laverne's eyes, but she understood watching her husband's attentiveness to Larry. Hugging her son, she replied, "I understand why you want to leave, and yes, I'll miss you." Michael Sr. and Larry were oblivious to the exchange between mother and son.

16 COUNT DOWN TO FREEDOM

The days and weeks went by amazingly fast for the Grayeson household. Larry and Michael II studied hard to maintain their high grades as they submitted college applications. In late April, both received letters from several colleges.

The University of Southern California accepted Michael II on a partial scholarship, to the family's delight. Michael Sr. was overjoyed when Cedar Valley University offered Larry a full scholarship, but Mrs. Grayeson had her doubt. She could not help wondering if her husband's excitement was due to Michael going far away or Larry staying close by.

Waves of emotions gripped her, and the boys as graduation approached. A week before graduation, Martin dropped by the Grayeson's home. Michael Sr. was shocked to see the man at his doorstep. Out of courtesy and curiosity, he invited the judge into the house.

"Mr. Grayeson, apologies for dropping by unannounced. I need to speak to you and your wife about Larry. Is she home?" He spoke as soon as he entered the hallway.

"Yes, she is home. One second." He told him, and then he called out for his wife, "sweetie, Laverne."

"Yes, what is it?" She yelled back.

"We have a visitor. Can you come into the living room now?" He responded.

Laverne, feeling annoyed with his interruption, entered the room. Her facial expression displayed her surprise at seeing the judge in her home.

"Judge Canister, to what do we owe this pleasure." She spoke as she composed herself.

"Sorry to barge in on you both like this. As you know, Ms. Washington is making great improvements; however, she cannot make the required decision. Is Larry at home?" He inquired before continuing.

"No, he is not. Did you need to speak to him?" The protective father asked.

Judge Canister wanted to remain anonymous, so he carefully crafted the information he was delivering to the family. "No, I do not need to speak to him. It is a delicate situation, so I am glad he is not here. Let me get to the point; Larry's father, who wants to remain unnamed, contacted the court. He had set up a college fund for the boy, and payment should go directly to the school of his choice. I believe that neither the boy nor the man knows each other, and the man cannot reveal himself. Hence the need for secrecy. My job is to locate the name of the chosen college so the trust can release the funds. Has he chosen a school?" The judge asked them.

A brief shock and happiness came over Michael Sr. for Larry. Knowing the scholarship Larry received would pay for the school fees, he wondered what would become of the funds. Pushing aside the idea that Larry's father could be a distraction to his career plan, he informed the judge of Larry's acceptance to the school where he worked. The judge obtained the direct number of the school and was about to leave when Michael stopped him. "By the way, Larry got accepted on full scholarship, so does that mean the funds will remain in the trust you mentioned." Mr. Grayeson asked out of curiosity.

"Scholarship, that's good news. I presume the school will send him the money if there is credit on the account; that is my best guess. I cannot comment for sure, as my instructions were to gather the school's information for them to send the check. I cannot see any reason for them not to release the funds." Martin explained, trying to distance himself from the topic.

"That makes sense. Thanks for giving us the heads up." Michael told him.

The curious mother could not hold it in anymore and exclaimed, "Forgive me if this is not my place, but you seem very devoted to the welfare of Larry and his mother. Why is that?"

Caught off guard, Martin quickly offered the best response he knew. "It is no secret that my wife's careless actions put the mother in the hospital. Since she could not make amends, I decided to pay Ms. Washington's medical bills and look after the boy's welfare where I could. When I saw the father's request, I knew it had to be me who did it. In case you are wondering, I do not know the father's name either." He told them before walking out the door. Even though he hated lying to the family, he justified his action by reiterating it was necessary.

The judge was unaware that the Grayeson family did not know who committed the crime. Both Laverne and Michael Sr. looked at each other in disbelief. "At least he's trying to do right by her and her son." She told her husband. Closing the door felt like she was ending another chapter in the ever-evolving saga of Sidney and Larry's life.

"The best words out of his mouth were about Larry getting money for school. I am sure the young man would be pleased about that." Her husband chimed in.

"Hmm, it will be difficult to tell a young man that he is getting money back from his college because someone paid it but not by whom. I think it would only open wounds we have yet to know. Let the judge and the school manage it and let him concentrate on studying and football. I am afraid if the subject of his father comes up, it might derail both your plans." Laverne knew her husband hung his hope on Larry's football career and dangling the idea of it disappearing was the only way she knew how to keep him from telling Larry what the judge wanted to remain confidential. Seeing sense in his wife's explanation, the man sighed loudly before returning to the list of athletes in his hand.

For the remainder of the week, the Grayeson household was chaotic but in an exciting way. As the days passed, each family member's excitement grew as they considered the next chapter of their lives.

Michael II stood in his room and stared at the graduation gown hanging on his closet door. He knew the robe represented the final hurdle of his childhood. Walking across the stage to receive his high school diploma meant he was one step from freedom. Although he would miss his mother, he would be free, at least for a few years, from the rejection he felt from his father.

Meanwhile, Larry was in his room doing the same thing, staring at his gown, but with a different thought in mind. As he stared at the robe, he wished desperately that his mother could be in attendance.

She was out of her coma but not out of the hospital. Sitting on the bed, he remembered the judge asking him if there was anything he needed to let him know. The young man found the man's number and called him.

17 GRADUATION DAY

"Boys, boys, did you eat breakfast already. We are running out of time before we must leave. Make sure you have everything with you. Are you listening to me?" Laverne yelled down the hall.

"Yes." The two male voices yelled back.

Graduation day filled the Grayeson's home with joy. It was bittersweet for Laverne and Michael Sr., who knew this was the last chapter in the young men's childhoods. Shaking her head to push the tears in her eyes back, Laverne pulled a green spaghetti-strapped dress and white jacket out of the closet. Zipping it up halfway, she walked into the bathroom with her husband. As he zipped the dress the rest of the way, Laverne commented. "Can you believe it has been 18 years since we brought our son home? Now he is embarking on a new journey." Her words echoed in the bathroom.

Mr. Grayeson did not respond to his wife's comment. He felt pain thinking about his son traveling across the country to attend school. However, he took solace in knowing Larry would remain in the house for at least another year. The parents, dressed and ready, wait by the door for the handsomely dressed young men. They walked proudly to the car with their cap and gown in hand.

Larry's relationship with Michael never returned as he had hoped. He did his best to involve his foster brother in every conversation or activity, but Michael would either decline or make a half-committed attempt to be involved. "Wow, are you excited about our graduation?" Larry asked him as the car backed out of the garage.

"Yep, I can't wait to get out of here," Michael responded, looking out the car window.

No matter how hard Laverne tried, she could not break the tension between her son and the other men in the house. The family arrived at the graduation hall on time. Climbing out of the car, Larry excused himself from the others to look for Martin. His guardian thought he wanted to find his friends until they saw him walking to the stairs where the judge stood waiting.

Martin saw Larry approaching and met him halfway. "Hello, are you excited about today?" He asked, trying to make small talk.

"Yes, I am, thank you." The young man spoke politely to the judge.

"I stopped by the hospital to see your mother last night. She is doing well and wishes she could have been here today. I told her about your request to videotape the event for you and her to watch later. She was happy about the idea. Where do you want me to sit?" Martin asked his son. Being at the graduation meant more to the man than Larry had imagined. After confirming the boy was his, he never thought he would be experiencing this life-changing event with him.

"I do not know the best place, but I was hoping you could sit with my other parents. I am sure momma Laverne will find the best seat." He responded.

Agreeing to follow the Grayeson's instructions on the seating arrangements, Martin and Larry met up with the family as they walked into the building. Since the students would assemble in a different location for entry into the ceremony, the boys bid goodbye and left the three adults. "I think it's wonderful that you would agree to videotape the ceremony." Laverne was the first one to break the awkward silence.

"Although I was surprised when he called me, I understood the importance of today. Shall we find a good seat?" Martin spoke as he extended his left hand toward the seating area. His mission was to record the graduation without engaging in any conversation that would prompt the family to ask more questions.

The graduation ceremony was long and comical, but the attendees made it to the end. The guardian and judge waited outside and watched the joyful students as they exited the building with sounds of cheers and laughter in celebration of their new achievements.

The adults observed as the graduates gathered in various groups to hug and take pictures. Laverne noticed Michael II shifting several times to avoid taking photographs with Larry. Seeing his mother's facial expression, the young man walked over to Larry to take a few pictures. The smile on her face encouraged him that he had done the right thing.

The two young men made their way to take photos with their

family. Martin's last duty was taking a family picture of the Grayeson. He used his camera to take a picture of Larry for his mother and a short video message from each family member to uplift Sidney as she continued to recover.

Later in the evening, the Grayson joined friends and a few family members at a restaurant to celebrate the students. The chatter and praises felt good to Michael II, and his attention changed as the thought of him leaving became a reality. "Are you excited about California?" John, his paternal uncle, asked as he leaned over and whispered.

"I was, but I am having second thoughts. I will not know anyone in California, and it is getting a little scary for me." He told the older man.

"Look, there is nothing wrong with being scared. When I went to Nebraska, I did not know anyone, and now I have friends, that beautiful woman across the table (pointing at his wife), and new family members. The beginning is scary, but everything will fall into place if you stay focused on your studies." John told him.

The young nephew appreciated the advice of his uncle. Looking around the table, he felt no one would miss him when he was gone. His feeling gave him peace with his decision. The family finished their meal then everyone returned to their homes.

18 FORGING AHEAD TO THE FUTURE

Moving to a new city was exciting and terrifying, yet Michael II was determined to succeed in his new Journey. The trip to Los Angeles, California, consisted of short sightseeing stops. The family arrived a day before the designated arrival date set by the dormitory, so Laverne booked two rooms for them to stay overnight. She realized any little setback could unnerve her son and decided to make light of the situation. Worn out from the trip, the family went to bed after eating dinner.

Michael II woke early in the morning with a sick feeling in his stomach. He was so mad at his dad that he never considered living independently. Knowing it was his first time away from his parents made him sick in the toilet. He showered before meeting them in the dining room for breakfast. The conversation started pleasantly before Michael Sr. began messaging Larry, which changed the mood.

"Dad, can you give me these last couple of hours without me having to share your attention." The young man spoke while shaking his head.

Laverne arrived at the table with her food in the middle of Michael's request to his dad. Sitting down, she told her husband in a soft voice, "really. Can we not get through breakfast without any incidents? Why can't you be in the moment with your son?"

Michael Sr. did not understand the fuss about him checking on Larry. "I am only making sure he's okay." He told them in an annoyed tone.

As Laverne opened her mouth to speak, her son stopped her. "It's okay, mom; let's eat to get this over with."

Hearing his son's comment, Michael Sr. attempted to explain his actions. Unfortunately, his son was no longer interested. Still feeling annoyed, Mr. Grayeson shrugged his shoulders.

The three of them ate in silence. The first-year college student felt alone and disappointed when he received a message from Dr. Brown. Reading her words of encouragement, he immediately felt better about his decision. Smiling, he playfully winked at his mother and handed her the pager. After reading the message, Laverne appreciated Dr. Brown's involvement in her son's life.

Thirty minutes later, the family arrived at the dormitory to move Michael into his room. Since he did not have a roommate, Laverne rearranged the dorm-provided furniture to make Michael comfortable. Standing in the middle of the room, Michael felt the jitters in his stomach again, except this time it was a joyous feeling.

Laverne and Michael Sr. spent several hours walking around the campus with their son. Young Michael's excitement increased when he saw the medical lab, and he could not wait to start. Exchanging hugs and tears, the parents left the new college student so he could settle in.

The student sat in his dorm room to assess his new living environment. He walked through the hall to get a sense of the students on the floor. Satisfied with what he saw, Michael returned to the medical lab to speak with the professor. Although he would not be eligible to work in the lab until his sophomore semester, he wanted to get acquainted with as many staff members as possible. Quickly, he found Dr. Gomez, a friend of Dr. Brown, and received an invitation to join the med student's weekly group meeting.

Meanwhile, in New Jersey, Larry walked through the university doors with great anticipation. Two months later, he arrived at football practice nervous and excited. As a first-year wide receiver, he did not expect to participate with the sophomores or seniors. Coach Rattington, who followed Larry's career through high school, put him in the game. His performance surprised both the coaches and the players. Feeling proud of his foster son, Michael Sr. could not resist boasting to everyone who would listen.

At first, staying home without Michael II felt weird for Larry, but he was happy to have Laverne and his mother for comfort. However, Laverne suffered in silence as she made Larry feel at home while missing her son. She knew it was not the perfect situation but speaking to Michael every week helped cheer her up on the bad days. Tired of him using the dormitory hall phone, she bought him a cellular phone and shipped it to him. The phone was cumbersome, but it meant she could speak to him anytime.

To maintain his secret identity, Martin continued to use the school to give Larry money without raising suspicion. Larry was surprised when he received a letter from the school informing him of a refund check. Larry purchased his first car five months after picking up the first check. Being mobile allowed him to visit his mother in between classes and practices.

Sidney's recovery increased significantly. Her recovery prompted the doctors to transfer her to a rehabilitation center. Learning to walk and using her hands were part of Sidney's rehab journey, and she was determined to fight through the pain and tears. Martin visited Sidney every week to rekindle her love for him. Sidney slowly began to lean on Martin's presence to keep her company between Larry's visits.

Michael Sr. refused to engage in any conversation about Sidney or her progress. He secretly feared Larry would return home with his mother. So, the older man spent many hours with Larry to keep him focused on playing and on him as a father figure. He was so engrossed with being a football dad that he lost sight of his son in California. Nevertheless, Laverne traveled back and forth through the first year of young Michael's college life.

Thanksgiving was Michael's first holiday away from his family because he decided to stay at school to avoid being around his father. When Dr. Brown heard he would be spending Thanksgiving alone, she placed a call to her friend, Dr. Gomez. Following the professor's insisting on his presence, the young man arrived at the house an hour early.

Standing at the door, Michael hesitated before ringing the bell. As he was about to put his finger on the buzzer, Dr. Gomez opened the solid oak door before opening the screen door. "I was wondering how long you were going to stand out there. I know our fall weather is warmer than New Jersey, but it is no excuse to stay outside." The teacher slapped the student's back as he entered the house.

"I thought maybe I was too early, so I was trying to shave off some time," he responded.

"Nonsense, you are on time. Let me round up the family into the dining room. Honey, our guest is here." He called out to his wife as he stretched his right hand out to collect Michael's jacket.

Ashley Gomez walked into the hallway area by the stairs to greet Michael. "It is nice to meet you. My husband says you were ambitious, but he never mentioned handsome. Wait until Ruby sets eyes on you." She spoke before returning to the kitchen.

As Michael stood in the living room, Dr. Gomez yelled for his children, "Ruby, Alex, and Shavon get down here now." The younger children, Alex, and Shavon raced down the stairs while Ruby made a dramatic entrance. She was upset with her father until she locked eyes with Michael. Her mother was right. The girl became entranced with the visitor.

Her eyes traveled from his eyes, lips, neck, and body down to his feet. Making her way to the bottom of the stairs, she walked in his direction. After formal introductions were over, the family sat at the dinner table. Ruby chose to sit directly across from Michael, who began sweating underneath his shirt and pants. His heart raced every time he looked into her eyes. To keep from leaving a puddle where he sat, he conversed with Mrs. Gomez about the food.

The guest of honor was excited when Alex began talking about his classmates, and laughter filled the room. Michael refused to look across the table at the glossy brown eyes and full lips of the young woman who sat there. At the end of the dinner, everyone pitched in to clean up. Looking at the time, Michael expressed his gratitude for a good evening. Instantly, Ruby volunteered to walk him to the car he got as a birthday gift from his mother. Smiling to himself, he accepted her offer as she slipped a piece of paper into his pocket and whispered, "call me later."

19 I'M SORRY IS TOO LATE

Michael II waited three days before calling Ruby because he wanted her father's permission beforehand. Above all, Michael's education was the most important thing in his life. If dating the professor's daughter jeopardized his chances, he would forgo the relationship. Arranging to meet the professor at the coffee shop near the campus, he expressed his intentions and asked for permission.

Dr. Gomez appreciated the young man's thoughtfulness and consideration of his feelings regarding his daughter. The father gave his approval for Michael to court Ruby but advised they should take it slow. Because the approach was sincere, Dr. Gomez was honest with his student about his daughter's shortcomings. "Son, thank you for speaking to me candidly about your intentions towards my daughter. It means a lot, but I must warn you. My daughter is intense and demanding. She does not understand the difference between your passion for studying and avoiding her. She breaks up with every boy within months because they would not spend every waking moment with her. I am telling you this so you can choose wisely. If you decide to pursue my daughter, be careful. I love my daughter very much, so don't say I did not warn you."

Michael's eyes opened a little wider. He had not expected such honesty from a father. "Thanks, I think, for sharing. I will lay my cards on the table and let her decide. My goal is to finish university and attend medical school, and I will not allow anyone to detour me from my goal, not even a beautiful girl." He told him.

"Glad to hear it. So that you know, dating my daughter won't give you any special treatment next year when you are in my class." Dr. Gomez told him.

"You mean I won't have to wait for two years? Wow, it's the best news I've heard today besides your permission, of course." The young man responded.

"We decided to make first-year students wait until their sophomore year because we had many of them drop out in the middle of the semester because they could not manage the course load. Before long, we realized they weren't sure about their majors when they started. You seem determined, and listening to you in our group discussions, I am sure you will do the work. I will speak to the administrator so they can open the class for your next school year." He told him.

Michael thought the Thanksgiving holiday turned out better than expected. On the third day after meeting Ruby, he called her after his last class. The young woman, who did not appreciate his lack of response to her command, got upset when he did not call her immediately after leaving her home. Looking at the number, she answered, "Hello."

"Hello, Ruby, it's Michael." He told her.

"Michael who." She snapped, being sarcastic.

"I guess I'll hang up since you don't remember me." He told her.

"Suit yourself." She answered, expecting his comments were part of a joke.

However, Michael had no intentions of playing games with her. "Okay, bye." He said before hanging up.

Within minutes, Ruby called him back. It was the first time someone challenged her and did not fall for her tactics. Michael allowed the phone to ring three times before answering. "Hello, so you remember me now?"

"Yes, I remembered you. I can't believe you hung up the phone." She told him.

"Since it would be a waste of my time and the person on the other end, there's no point in me speaking to someone who doesn't know or remember me." He pointed out to her.

"You have a point." She answered.

As he contemplated asking her to dinner, she questioned his delay in contacting her. "What took you so long to call me?" Hearing her demanding question, young Michael chose not to answer directly; instead, he asked a different question.

"Would you like to go out for some pizza on Friday? I have a half-day, so I should be free at 3 PM. We can talk about return calls then."

His response was not what she expected.

She pulled the receiver from her face, looked at it for a few seconds, then answered. "Sure, I would love to go." Agreeing to eat at a pizzeria was rare for Ruby. Normally, she demanded to eat at a fancy restaurant, but somehow, she knew he was different.

Her voice softened, and Michael used the moment to ask an intimate question. "So, do your lips always look kissable, or was it due to your lipstick?"

Blushing at the question, she answered, "I do not wear lipstick. For your information, I only wear lip gloss. I guess you will have to wait until Friday to see if they are kissable or not." Chuckling at the response, he agreed it would be fun to find out on Friday.

Michael and Ruby spoke for a few more minutes before returning to his studies. Later that evening, Michael's phone rang, and recognizing the house phone, he answered immediately. "Hello," He expected his mother to be on the other line.

"Hello," Michael Sr. returned the greeting. Hearing the male voice on the other line startled the student because it was unexpected. Mr. Grayeson's son did not know what to say.

"How are you doing in California?" The father asked.

"Fine." His son's answer was short and cold.

"I wanted to see how you were doing. I am sorry you did not make it home for the turkey holiday. We did nothing big or fancy, but I wanted you to know we missed you." Michael Sr. expressed to his son in a cheerful tone.

"Glad you all did something. I had a great evening with the Gomez family. Dr. Gomez is such a good father, and he knew how to make everyone feel at home and included." He responded, directing his comments at his father's treatment of him.

"Look, son, I don't want to argue with you. I know I've been focused on other areas, so I wanted to say I am sorry." The older Michael's voice sounds like he was close to tears.

"'I am sorry' is a bit too late, don't you think? I am in the middle of studying for my test. Was there anything else you wanted?" Young Michael's tone remained cold and icy.

"No, son, I don't think it's too late to say I am sorry. When are you coming home?" He asked.

"When are you coming to California?" That was the response he gave to his father.

"Fair point. How about mom and I come for Christmas? Would that work for you?" Michael Sr. tried to appeal to the voice on the other end of the phone.

"I am good with whatever." Michael II answered. Secretly he hoped they did come to visit because he missed his mom. Even though he tried not to involve her, he knew his defiance with his dad hurt her.

"Then it's settled. Your mother will make the arrangements, and we'll see you then. Bye, son."

"Bye, dad." After the call ended, young Michael sat in his mesh back rolling chair and stared at the phone. The call was unexpected and left him wondering why. He thought about phoning his mother to inquire but fought against it. Returning to his studies, he put it out of his mind for now.

Laverne sat next to her husband as he apologized to their son. She had encouraged him earlier in the day to make amends. Her action came after she visited Sidney at the rehabilitation center and learned she would be going home before Christmas. Seeing the excitement on Larry's face meant he would be joining her. The dutiful wife relayed the conversation to her husband. Michael Sr. was disappointed, yet he knew it would have happened eventually.

Larry Martin was thrilled with the news of his mother going home. He was unsure how he felt about the judge getting close to her, but his mother's happiness meant a lot. Seeing her smile and joke with the older man was bittersweet. In the end, Larry was happy to return home with his mother. It did not take long for him to talk with his foster father. He appreciated everything the man did for him, but it was time to be there for his mother. Seeing the sadness in Mr. Grayeson's eyes, he asked if he could still be there for his games and practice. It did give a little glimmer of hope for the football fanatic father.

20 IT'S THE SEASON FOR CHANGE

The days passed swiftly for the families as they made plans for the Christmas season. Larry returned home with his mother the second week of December, and Michael II continued to take it slow with Ruby. Dr. Gomez marveled at how different his daughter behaved with Michael. It was as though he transformed the young woman into a new person.

During their many conversations over the phone and on their dates, Michael encouraged Ruby to go back to school to obtain her cosmetology certificate. She often expressed her desire for hair and make-up but felt she was not good enough. Listening to how enthusiastic she spoke about the topic, he challenged her to try. He promised her he would not mention it again if it did not work out. Taking on the challenge, she applied and was accepted to one of Los Angeles's best schools. Ruby's friends and family were pleased to watch her slowly change from a selfish girl to a well-rounded, caring woman. They credited her growth with Michael's association.

Christmas week, Laverne arrived in California with her husband to visit their son. The weather was beautiful, and as the wind blew softly, it gently lifted her hair off her face. "Wow, what a difference compared to New Jersey. I could get used to this. What do you think?" She asked her preoccupied husband.

"Eh, it is okay, but not for me. You know I like to see the seasons change." He responded, looking around for his son.

Michael II pulled up to the sidewalk where his parents were waiting at the airport. Jumping out of his gray Volkswagen Jetta, he hugged his mother and shook his father's hand. After putting the two suitcases in the trunk, he drove them to the hotel.

The silence in the car was deafening, so Laverne made small talk. Finally, she found a topic they both loved, food. Each of the men expressed their desire for a good Christmas dinner. After checking in, Michael II went to their hotel room with his parents and then informed them of the dinner plans.

"By the way," he started as he sat on the tan-colored armchair. "Dr. Gomez invited us to Christmas dinner, and mom, I want you to meet Ruby. She is the girl I have been seeing."

"You mean the same doc you went to for Thanksgiving dinner? I thought we were dining as a family." Michael Sr. tried to hide his jealousy as he remembered his son's comments about the man.

"Don't be silly. That is a lovely idea, and we will still be eating as a family. I cannot wait to meet this, Ruby. What can you tell me about her? This way, I am not surprised when I meet her." Laverne spoke to her son as she raised her left eyebrow out of curiosity.

"Mom, you are not going to shrink the girl. Please leave your professional opinion at the door and be a mom when you meet her." Michael II had never been as serious with a girl as with Ruby. Laverne was concerned that he was falling too fast. Deep down, she wished he had dated more, to be sure. However, she respected his ability to choose who complements him. "Okay, I'll try." She gave in, looking at the seriousness of his facial expression.

Michael stayed with his parents a few more hours before returning to campus. It felt good having both their attention, yet he began to think about Larry. Sadly, he refused to ask because he feared it would give his father an excuse to focus elsewhere.

Christmas in Los Angeles was nothing like Christmas in New Jersey, and Michael Sr had mixed feelings about the atmosphere. He woke up around 7 a.m. and traveled to the banquet hall for breakfast with his wife. The hotel's decorative table settings and festive meals sparked a feeling of the season. Piling the various breakfast meats of sausage, bacon, and ham with eggs on one plate, he took a second plate for his French toast and Danishes.

Laverne chuckled at him because she knew he was excited. After putting some bacon and a spoon full of scrambled eggs onto her plate, she spotted the waffle maker. Grabbing the attention of a hotel banquet staff, she poured the batter on the waffle griddle. Moments later, the young man carried two hot, fluffy waffles with maple syrup to her table.

Soon after finishing their meal, the couple returned to the room to plan the remainder of the day. Around 10:30 am, Michael II arrived at the hotel to take his parents around town. His mother was extremely proud of her son. Out of curiosity, she asked, "Michael dear, have you made any friends since you've been here?"

Michael II looked at his mother and shook his head. "Mom, of course, I made friends. You do not think I just study nonstop, do you?"

"Do not be mad; she's asking because she knows that everything else gets blocked out when you focus on one thing. We want to make sure you are enjoying college." His father added.

Hearing his father's concern for him was a welcome surprise for the young man.

Escorting them out of the hotel, he decides to change the topic of discussion from his personal life to theirs. "So, how is it being an empty nester? I am sure you too are finding ways to be teenagers again, like chasing each other around the house."

Michael's question made his mother blush. "Junior, that's grown-up business right there. You do not want to know the answer, trust me." Michael Sr spouted as if to shield his wife.

Everyone burst into laughter, and it made Laverne incredibly happy. It set the stage for a successful tour of the local areas.

The next day everyone woke up excited because it was Christmas. The Grayeson family met for breakfast and exchanged gifts. Later, Michael II returned to the hotel to pick up his parents for dinner. Traveling time to Dr. Gomez's house was 45 minutes with traffic. As she thinks about meeting the woman who appeared to have captured her son's heart, Laverne's anticipation increases.

Parking in the driveway, young Michael reminded his mother to be on her best behavior. The family of three stood at the home entrance waiting for someone to answer. Laverne was about to ring the bell again when Alex opened the door.

"Hi, Michael and Michael's parents. Come in. Daddy went to the store, and mommy is in the kitchen." He spoke as he welcomed them in.

"Hi, Alex. Mom and dad, this is Alex, the younger of three Gomez clans. Alex, these are my parents, Laverne and Michael."

"Wow, you have the same name. How cool is that? Mommy, we have guests." He yelled.

Ashley rushed out of the kitchen with flour in her hair to greet the

Grayeson family. "Hello, I am Ashley. Sorry I was not at the door to welcome you. We had a mishap in the kitchen, and I have been working hard to recreate the dishes." She told them as she extended her left hand as soon as she finished wiping it with the towel hanging from her apron's pocket.

"It is quite all right. I understand. Is there anything I can help you with?" Laverne offered to be polite.

"No, nonsense, you are our guest. Please have a seat Tomás and Ruby will be back soon, then we can eat." Ashley told them.

Walking back into the kitchen, she told her son to take the family to the formal living room. Following behind the boy, Michael Sr. was surprised to see the many football and baseball paraphernalia lined the wall. "Are these yours, Alex?" He asked.

"The baseball trophies are mine, but all the football stuff belongs to my dad and my sister Shavon." He told the older Michael.

"Did your sister get a trophy for cheerleading? How interesting." Michael Sr. told him because he could not picture a girl playing football.

"You are funny. No, my sister is not a cheerleader; she played in the game." Alex laughed.

"What, a girl is playing football. What is this world coming to?" He asked rhetorically.

"The times are changing, love. Women's equality is not just in the boardroom but also on the field." Laverne answered.

"It's just not right; that's all I am saying." Mr. Grayeson spoke aloud.

"She is surprisingly good at running the ball. Dad always gets excited when she is on the field, but momma is terrified." Alex told them as he leaned against the arm of the light blue sofa.

The little banter about whether girls should play football continued until Ruby and Mr. Gomez returned home. Hearing the door open, Alex ran to let them know their guests had arrived. Excited to see Michael, Ruby walked quickly into the formal living room. "Hi Mikey, I am so glad you came." She told him as she gave him a hug and a peck on the cheek. Normally she kissed him passionately on the lips, but she wanted to respect his parents. Dr. Gomez entered the room not long after Ruby to greet the family.

It was an hour later when everyone, except Shavon, sat down to eat. Michael Sr. was intrigued by the young lady playing football and wanted to speak to her and voiced his disappointment of her not being there. Dr. Gomez said a prayer of thanksgiving over the food, and everyone began to put the various food on their plates.

21 INACCURATE JUDGMENT

The conversation around the table was pleasant and light. Prejudging the family, Laverne assumed that Ashley was a stay-at-home mother. She asked, "so do you enjoy staying at home now that the children are older?" Her question was insulting Mrs. Gomez.

Clearing her throat, Ashley asked, "what do you mean by me staying at home?" to clarify the question. She did not want Michael's mother to feel uncomfortable, but she would not allow her to insult her either.

"I am sorry. Everything is so immaculate, and you were cooking all this meal; I assumed you were a stay-at-home mom, but I should have known better." Laverne apologizes.

"Everyone pitches in around the house. There are no prima donnas in here." Ashley responded.

Dr. Gomez knew his wife would not comment on her achievements, so he always did it for her. "My wife is very humble. She does not like to brag about herself, but she is an accomplished neuroscientist with a minor degree in physics. Even though her day consists of research and clinical trials on patients with neurological issues, she still finds time to take care of her family at night. She is a better doctor than I am." He told them.

"That is quite an accomplishment." Michael Sr. stated.

"Yes, it is." Dr. Gomez responded.

Laverne carefully chose her words as she began to converse with Ruby. Her questions came across as judgmental to Ashley. Although she wanted to interject, she appreciated her daughter's ability to defend herself. Feeling the chill at the table, Laverne asked, "my

Michael is studying hard to be a sports doctor and with both your parents being doctors, are you following that path as well?"

Ruby did not know if Laverne was throwing shade with her question. Confidently she answered, "my mom and dad are great with studying and all that book stuff, but it is not for me. I want to work with my hands and make people beautiful. At first, I did not know what I wanted to do because everyone expected me to be like my parents, except Michael. He wants me to be whatever makes me happy." She spoke while looking at Michael longingly.

"It is great that you want to make people beautiful. Some women do hair and makeup, so is that what you want to do?" Michael Sr. asked. In his mind, it was in line with his expectation of a woman's career.

"Yes, it is." She responded.

Sensing the awkward conversation, Michael II asked Dr. Tomás how he met his wife. It changed the mood of the conversation as the doctor began to reflect on when he met Dr. Ashley for the first time. His story was almost identical to young Michael and Ruby's early relationship. Putting the final piece of roast pork in his mouth, the father of three placed the knife and fork on the plate and began speaking.

"When I met Ashley, I had no clue what to do with my life. I was scared to ask her out because she was incredibly determined and well-mannered. At first, she questioned my motives, but I remained honest with her. She was not buying my answers. Luckily, I had worn her down, and she said yes.

The first real conversation between us was intense. The kids' mother grilled me about my future like a police officer interrogating me. In the end, I went home and reassessed my life. The second time she allowed me to take her out, she began with a simple question "what is your first love?" I never had anyone ask me about my first love before, and I immediately thought the question was about a person." He told them.

"Was she asking you about a woman daddy?" Ruby asked.

"Nope, she was asking about my passion, which happens to be football. I played football from the age of six until college. Honestly, I was good but not good enough for the NFL. Graduating from college with a business degree did not make me happy. It did not take long for me to enroll at the University of Southern California and get my medical degree to wrap the story up. I practiced for a few years before returning as a professor. If it were not for her persistence and pushing me, I would not be the man I am today. That is why I am so proud of you, Michael. You know what you want, and you pushed my daughter to find her passion. Did I wish she followed us? Of course, but she must follow her dreams." He concluded the story.

Laverne looked quizzically at her son. Although she understood what Dr. Gomez was trying to convey, she did not think it was her son's job to motivate their daughter. Dr. Ashley Gomez smiled at her husband's story while studying Laverne's facial expression. She agreed with his account and added how important it is for both parties in a relationship to motivate one another. As the family ate, they continued to swap stories.

In the end, both families felt the dinner was successful. The children cleaned the table and washed the dishes. While they were gathering the plates and bowls, Dr. Tomás offered a cigar and glass of cognac to Michael Sr. and escorted him to the newly renovated man cave. Entering the room, the older Michael was amazed and jealous at the same time. He admired the projector tv, mini bar, wine refrigerator, and the two cozy brown leather recliners with a sofa between them. His mouth opened to comment when he saw the keg station in the corner of the room. "Wow, this is a great setup you have here. It is more impressive that your wife allowed you to build this because I do not think mine would go for it." Mr. Grayeson finally forced the words out of his mouth.

"This," pointing around the room, "was not easy. It took me years to convince the misses to let me change the garage into a man cave. However, her objection remained the same every year because she did not want to park outside. One day we saw a commercial for a custom-built shed, and I called and asked if they could attach it to the house. It turned out building to my specification would depend on me obtaining a permit and having space." He started telling Michael as they sat in the recliners.

"I guess it's obvious you had what you needed to build it." The Athletic Director told him.

"I had the space but needed to get the permit. We waited months to hear back from the county. When I finally got the approval, I felt like a kid again. The actual build did not take long, and here we are now, enjoying this cozy space. This place is my escape from the craziness. Do they offer something like this in New Jersey?" Dr. Gomez's extended the footrest on the chair to relax.

Sitting in the right recliner, Michael released his footrest following the homeowner, then responded to Dr. Gomez's comment. "Even if they did, we don't have space on our property for an addition."

The sadness in the man's voice gave Dr. Gomez pause. "Now, that is a shame. You're welcome to hang here whenever you visit." He finally offered.

"Now you're talking." The older Michael stated.

Amid the men relaxing and the kids cleaning, Ashley invited Laverne to join her in the family room. Ashley pointed to the gray plush sofa and handed her a Kahlua coffee. "I am impressed with your accomplishments," Laverne told her.

"Not bad for a housewife." Ashley laughed.

It was clear to Laverne her previous statement ruffled the woman's feathers. She quickly responded, "I know I came across as judgmental, but that is not how I am normally. I let my psychiatric knowledge and parental protective nature override my common sense. Please accept my apology."

Ashley accepted the apology and changed the conversation to discuss their children's relationship. The neuroscientist continued to pay attention to Laverne's facial expression. To her surprise, the smile on the woman's face seemed genuine. They exchanged their hopes for the future, then Laverne spotted the vast collection of records in the glass cabinet. "What kind of music do you like?" Sliding out of the comfortable sofa, Ashley pulled out a Miles Davis album and put it on the record player.

The ladies listened to the music as they finished drinking their coffee. Although the Grayeson family enjoyed relaxing with the Gomez at their home, it was time to leave. Exchanging pleasantries, Michael II drove his parents to the hotel.

The next day, Michael and Laverne prepared to return to New Jersey. Throughout his visit, Michael Sr. was secretly messaging Larry. He was careful in his communication after the disapproval from his son the last time he was in California. Climbing into the car, Mr. Grayeson expressed how proud he was of his son, making Michael II happy.

22 CONDITIONAL LOVE

The years passed rapidly for Michael and Larry, who made great strides in school. In his senior year of college, Larry, the starting wide receiver for his college, caught the attention of several football scouts. Michael II's contribution to various projects in the school did not go unnoticed by the university's trustees. Michael Sr. found himself in another conflict of interest when his son and Larry had an event during the same time.

The final medical symposium was scheduled for the last week in April, the same time as the NFL draft event. Larry asked Mr. Grayeson to accompany him and his mother to the function without knowing that Michael II had made a similar request. Mr. Grayeson discussed the situation with his wife. He knew both events were important but felt the NFL draft ranked slightly higher than the medical program. However, Laverne expressed her disagreement and disapproval of putting anything before their son.

Michael II called his parents to finalize their travel plans when he learned only his mother would be in attendance. Laverne informed her son of his father's decision to attend the NFL draft with Larry. Her son was not surprised that his father would choose football over science. However, he thought they had moved past his obsession with football over the years, but he was wrong. Dismissing his father's decision, he confirmed his mother's flight information.

During the passing of each day, Michael Sr. never mentioned his son's conflicting event to Larry. Enthusiastic about being among other great football players, parents, and NFL staff members, he could not see anything else. Two days before the draft, a car arrived at the Grayeson home with Sidney and Larry to pick up Michael Sr. for the airport. Larry knew it was custom for Laverne to stand by the door and wish them off, but she was not there. As he was about to ask about her, Michael Sr. started asking questions.

Throughout the trip to the hotel, Larry felt something was off with his ex-foster father. Unfortunately, he did not get to confront the feeling with all the scheduled activities.

On the night of the events, Laverne, dressed in a dazzling black A-line high neck floor-length chiffon evening dress in California, could not wait to see her son. Michael II was proud to escort his mother and Ruby, who wore a knee-length off-the-shoulder gray dress with pearls. The young man felt special with both women on either side of his arms. The three mingled with the other guest before taking their seats.

To Laverne's delight, her son was one of the keynote speakers in the beautifully choreographed program. Michael, who wore a dark navy-blue suit with a creamed shirt and navy and striped cream tie, looked dashing standing behind the podium. "Isn't he simply gorgeous?" Ruby whispered to Laverne.

Chuckling at the young girl's comment, Mrs. Grayeson agreed with her. Listening to her son carefully presenting his research on sports medicine and the need for protective gear brought tears to her eyes. She was happy and sad at the same time. Although she was happy for her son, she was sad his dad did not experience their son's brilliance.

However, Mr. Grayeson was enjoying the spotlight surrounding Larry. He listened to the presentations and all the commentaries. As the first-round picks were over, his excitement died down a little. Larry's phone rang just as he was about to head to the restroom. He was so excited because it meant a team had drafted him. There were loud cheers at the table as Larry walked up to the podium to collect his team Jersey. Even though he missed out in round one, his mother was still extremely proud of him.

Both events wrapped up around the same time. In excitement, Larry called Michael II to give him the good news. He had known their relationship had gotten strange, but he desperately wanted to get his foster brother's approval. Before the speech, Michael II handed his phone to Laverne for safekeeping. It did not dawn on him to get it back when he returned to his seat. Michael's phone buzzed in her purse as they strolled down the street to enjoy the warm night's breeze. Reaching for it, she answered, not realizing it was her son's phone. "Hello, momma Laverne, is that you?" The voice on the other end called out.

"Hi Larry, yes, it's me." She replied.

"Wow, I did not know you were going to visit Michael. I thought it was strange you were not at the door when we picked up daddy Michael." He told her.

"Yes, dear. I am here because Michael's symposium is tonight. He did an excellent job as the keynote speaker." She informed him.

"Wait, what. Do you mean Michael had a function tonight as well? OMG, I did not know that. He must hate me thinking I took his dad away from him again. If I had known, I would never ask daddy Michael to come." The newly drafted football player began apologizing.

"Do not worry yourself about it. I am surprised you called, is everything all right?" She questioned him.

"Oh, I thought I called Michael's phone." He responded.

Pulling the phone from her ear, she noticed it did belong to her son. "You are right; it is his phone. Let me get him." She spoke.

Laverne muted the phone before handing it to her son. "He is reaching out to you, so be nice. He did not know you had a program tonight."

Michael II took the phone off mute and spoke to Larry. "Hey, what is going on? Did you get what you wanted?" His question was cynical.

"So sorry, bro. I truly did not know you had something special going on tonight. I was calling to tell you about the draft and that I got in, but now it seems stupid for me to call." Larry stated.

"Naw, it is not stupid. Congratulations on your win, man. I knew it was something you always wanted. Who knows, if I am not busy helping some of your athletic friends, I might attend one of your games." Michael congratulated his foster brother.

"Man, I truly feel so bad that Mr. Grayeson chose my draft program over yours, and it sucks," Larry told Michael.

This conversation was the first time since he was twelve years old that Larry called Michael Sr. by his surname. Now that he was older, he recognized the importance of being there for your family, the way his mother tried to show up for him. He could not imagine her choosing something or someone else over him. The two young men spoke for five more minutes before ending the call.

Larry returned to the room where his mother and Mr. Grayeson were waiting. He planned to attend the after-party; however, after hearing what transpired, he decided to disinvite Michael Sr. Sidney had already agreed to let the boys have a night on their own and knew Larry would rather hang out with Michael than with her. She credited the foster father for taking an interest in her son and molding him into the star he was.

She hugged her son and was about to say goodnight when she noticed the sadness in his eyes. "What's wrong, sweetie?" She asked.

Before Larry could answer, Michael Sr. interjected. "What could be wrong? He is an NFL player, and now he gets the chance to celebrate with his fellow draftees. I do not see anything to be sad about."

"You see, that is the problem. I bought into your dream of being a famous football star, and you love it so much that you would reject your son's program to attend this function. I am not sure if I am more disgusted at myself for not seeing it earlier or you for your actions." Larry told him as he stood by the window.

"Son, what are you talking about? I knew this was an important night for you, so I did not want to miss it. I support you, and I hope you know that." Michael did his best to smooth the young man's emotions.

"Again, another problem. I am not your son. I am a skinny boy that your son invited to dinner because I was hungry. You latched onto the notion of me loving football, and nothing else mattered. Your son, who carries your name, had an important event tonight that you thought was not worth attending because you wanted to be amongst football players. My mother fought with everything she had to come back to me. Mrs. Grayeson did all she could to include Michael and me, but you. All you ever did was mock his dreams and make him feel less of a person. When I asked you to attend with me, you could have told me about Michael's symposium. I would have encouraged you to go, and we would celebrate the outcome later. Instead, you chose for me. Tonight, I think I should spend time with my mother. I will see you in the lobby tomorrow for check out." Larry walked out the door with his mother as soon as he finished talking. He did not allow Mr. Grayeson to respond.

Larry tried to enjoy himself after the incident with his ex-foster father, but he could not. He escorted his mother back to her hotel room an hour later. Sidney could see the hurt in her son's eyes, and she wondered if he was hurting for Michael Sr. or Michael Junior.

Michael Sr. stood in the same spot in the hotel room for a while.

He could not comprehend what had occurred moments earlier. He struggled to understand why Larry would be upset about attending the draft rather than the symposium. Coming to his senses, he called his wife to let her know what had happened. The phone rang five times before going to voicemail. The older man stood in the hotel room with nothing but his thoughts.

The next morning, Michael and Larry had different experiences after their programs. Michael felt at ease as he took his mother out for breakfast, while Larry was still upset about not having a choice. The mothers, with care, spoke love to their sons. Around 11:00 am, Laverne boarded her plane to return home while Larry loaded the bags into the car. The journey back home was quiet for them all.

23 REDEMPTION

Samantha Canister walked out of the women's prison on a warm Thursday afternoon. Spending six years inside a small cell gave her a better perspective on life. Exiting the building, she wore the same blue shirt and black pants she had going in. Standing on the curbside, she had no one to meet her.

Unaware of Martin's plan, Samantha was on the verge of tears when a black town car pulled up in front of her. The driver asked her name after exiting the vehicle. Once she confirmed her identity, he opened the rear passenger side door for her to get in. climbing into the driver's side, he introduced himself as her driver hired to take her home.

"Home, that is a relative term." She mumbled to herself. The divorced woman had no idea where home was. Leaning her head on the car window, she wondered if the driver was taking her to the house, she had shared with Martin for most of her life.

Grievously, Martin did not inform her that he had sold the house. The driver pulled up to a brownstone duplex building. He handed her the envelope and house keys as instructed, then drove away. Samantha stood on the sidewalk dumbfounded. When she left her home, it was a beautiful white estate with six bedrooms and five and a half baths. The entire first floor was an open space so that she could enjoy the kitchen, living, and dining area from anywhere. She hosted lavished parties and meetings with her socialite friends, and now she is standing looking at an ugly brownstone building.

Wiping the tears from her face, she opened the black steel gate, walked up the stairs, opened the door, and entered. She was pleasantly surprised at the spaciousness and beauty of the home. The outside looks like a duplex, but the renovated inside changed from two separate apartments to a two-story house. She emptied the envelope's contents on the countertop and read the note.

"Dear Sam, I am pleased about your release from prison. After our divorce, I sold the house and bought you this place. I had it renovated to suit your taste. It might not be what you expect, but it is yours to do what you will. Per our arrangements, I have sent the monthly alimony to your bank account for the last six years. The enclosed check is my final payment, which is more than I originally agreed to. Sorry how it all turned out, but I encourage you to start new. I asked my colleagues to inquire about expunging your records, but I do not know if it will happen. Someone will contact you in the coming weeks with a response. Good luck and goodbye, Martin."

The note did not surprise Samantha because she knew he would be by Sidney's side after the divorce. The house was not what she would have chosen; however, she was too tired to complain. She found the large bedroom and the large walk-in closet walking up the stairs. "At least he had the decency to arrange my clothes the way I like them." She thought to herself.

Samantha smiled as she turned the water on to take a bath in the white clawfoot tub. Later in the evening, she found the grocery and the keys to her car hanging on the wall next to the refrigerator. "It's almost like he was trying to give me a smaller version of the home he took from me." She mumbled aloud.

Pushing the thoughts aside, she climbed onto the sofa and turned on the television. Early the next morning, she rose suddenly out of sleep, thinking she was dreaming about being free. Looking around the room several times, she realized it was real. She laid back down for a couple of hours before getting up, dressing, and driving to the store.

Samantha's actions did not take long to catch up to her. As she strolled down the quiet street, she bumped into Sidney, who was leaving the floral store. The meeting took both ladies by surprise. Sidney was aware of her attacker's release but never thought they would be face to face.

"Hello." Samantha was the first to speak.

"Hi," was all Sidney could muster up.

"I am the last person you want to speak to after all that has happened. You do not owe me anything, but I would like the chance to explain my actions." Martin's ex-wife told her.

"You are right, you are the last person I expect to run into, and I certainly do not owe you anything. Although you do not deserve the right to state your case to the person you have hurt, I will give you this opportunity as I do not intend on us speaking again."

The ladies crossed the street and sat at an outside table at the nearby coffee shop. Ordering a coffee for herself and motioning to Samantha to order her beverage, Sidney expressed her displeasure toward the woman. The coffee arrived within minutes, and then Ms. Canister began her speech to describe how sorrowful she felt.

"Before I begin, I want to apologize for my actions. I know nothing I could say can take away or make light of my crime. I was wrong, and I dutifully served my time." She started.

"All that sounds good, but why did you try to kill me?" Sidney interrupted her.

"When I met Martin, everything was wonderful. He made me feel so special and beautiful. We were good for a while; then he started changing. In the beginning, he had a certain sparkle in his eyes when he came home from 'long meetings.' Then he started traveling more and bringing back apology gifts. He began getting out of bed in the middle of the night and would spend hours in the bathroom. His absence from the home became increasingly, then the gifts stopped. I began following him to hotels and restaurants where he would meet you. I was angry, but I thought it was a fling that would fizzle out. I console myself thinking he would never leave me. That was until I followed him to the jewelry store. I did not see what he bought, but his face said it all. I sat in my car and watched him walk into the hotel. Hurt and broken, my instinct was to go home, pack my bags and take him for all he is worth." She told Sidney.

"I guess that plan did not work since you were still married to him. You loved him enough to hit me with your car and speed away." Sidney remarked cynically.

"You are right; it was my intention until I saw him storm out of the hotel and get in his car. The way he slammed the door meant his plans did not go as he expected. He held the steering wheel and shook it so hard that the car also shook. I watched the man cry like a baby, and all I could think of was, finally, it was over. I can get my husband back now. Unfortunately for me, I was wrong. His body was back, but not his heart or his emotions. Everything was robotic for him. We had sex when I initiated it, but there was nothing in it." Samantha's eyes looked glazed over as she remembered her past relationship with the Judge.

"So why did you stay if you knew he did not love you?" Miss. Washington asked.

"Because I thought my love was enough for the both of us. Then it happened on October 14; he walked into the house whistling. I stood by the bathroom door, watching him dance in the shower. When he looked at me, the sparkle was back. My heart sank because I knew that meant either you were back in his life, or he had found someone else. Stupidly, I followed him again. Everything was normal at first. He went to the gym, ran, and sat in the park. I thought he was having a midlife crisis. What a joke! I followed him to the skating rink. I felt foolish watching his car and was about to leave when he left the building. He sat in his car staring at the door, so I stayed. Who walked out the building, the woman from his past?" She told her, then took a sip of her coffee.

"I take it the woman from his past is me?" Sidney voiced.

"Yes – it is you. I could not believe it; to make it worse, you had a son. I wondered if that was his son and got my answer on Monday when I found the results in his desk drawer." Samantha's anger at Martin was evident to the woman sitting across from her.

"To be fair, he did not know he had a child. I could not locate him after finding out I was pregnant to let him know." She tried to reason with the distraught woman.

"Martin, not knowing about your son would have been okay if he had not talked me out of having a child of my own. Whenever the topic of children came up throughout our marriage, he would dismiss it. So, to find out he had a child and to watch him provide for that boy was just too much. I never intended to run you over when I got in my car that day. Something in me snapped when he stood at your table beaming with love, and I could see you trying to defuse the situation, but he could not help himself. Seeing you cross the street; I lost my sense of reality. I stupidly thought if I could make you go away, I could get my husband back. That did not work." She expressed her feelings to Sidney.

As the ladies finished their coffee, Samantha felt a sigh of relief, expressing herself to Sidney. Although her ex-husband's lover might not appreciate her explanation, it made her feel better. That meant more to her than Sidney's forgiveness. In the meantime, Sidney listened to her attacker's story and reasoning behind the attack, yet it did not make the recurring pain she feels from time to time go away.

Throughout the story, what emerged was Martin's love for her. The realization gave Larry's mother a unique perspective on letting Martin into her life on a personal level. "The difficulties you faced within your marriage were unfortunate. I was not aware Martin was married. If I had, there would not have been a relationship. It did not matter what he did or did not do; I should not have been the recipient of your anger. I lost crucial memorable moments with my son. I missed his senior year in school, prom, graduation, and the first couple of years in college. None of that I can get back because you wanted a man to love you. I hear you, but it does not change what you did or give me back my lost years.

I do have to thank you. I have kept Martin at arm's length since he tried to push himself back into my life. However, after listening to you, I may give him a chance. Now, I must complete my errands. I need to make dinner for my son. He is visiting, and I have no intention of missing any more time with him." Completing her statement, Sidney rose from her chair and walked away. Not waiting for Samantha to respond was her way of relinquishing control from the ex-Mrs. Canister. Samantha sat at the coffee shop for an hour before continuing her stroll. Hearing that Sidney would give Martin a chance at a relationship should have upset her, but it did not. She smiled at the thought that life was looking up for her.

24 DON'T ADJUST THINGS FOR ME

Entering professional football meant no more favoritism for Larry. He was face to face with men who were bigger and faster than he was. He knew he had to condition his body to secure his future as a footballer. He reconnected with Robert, Michael's cousin, who became a weightlifting coach. Several months into his training routine with other lifters, he added muscles and strength in his core, arms, and legs. His new body and confidence showed as he practiced with the team.

Michael II expressed his desire to treat people who chose sports as a career to news reporters covering the symposium. The interview slipped his mind until he received a call from the Randforth Clinic offering him a position. The clinic specializes in athletes' recovery. Michael knew this offer was just what he needed but did not want to seem desperate. He waited a week before responding with his acceptance.

On their 30th birthday, Michael II and Larry's mothers planned a joint surprise birthday party. Simultaneously, Michael made plans to propose to Ruby, and only Dr. Tomás Gomez knew his plan. As part of the surprise, Laverne called Ashley to arrange for the entire family to join the festivities. Since Michael was in California and Larry was in Arizona, the mothers found a venue in Blythe to bridge the gap.

Dr. Gomez thought the birthday party would impact the wedding plans, and he wondered how he could ensure the proposal happened on schedule without spoiling the surprise. Carefully choosing his words, he inquired if Michael was still considering the proposal. They walked through the plans but with a twist. Michael mentioned his mother suggesting the family visit Blythe for his birthday.

Effortlessly, the doctor offered to change his plans as well. Michael felt he was inconveniencing his future in-laws. "Please do not adjust your plans for me. I am sure I can talk my mother into pushing our trips to another day."

Catastrophic horror flashed across the panic-stricken doctor's face of Michael's decision's impact on everyone if he postponed his trip. He quickly had another solution. "Did you say your mom wants to go to Blythe? Funny, that is a place I have never visited before. Do you think she would mind if we tagged along?"

"Now that sounds like a great idea. My mother's presence when I asked Ruby to marry me would make it special. Thanks for suggesting it. I will talk to my mom later today." Michael responded.

It had been years since Michael Sr. saw his son and Larry. The thought of having them in the same room to celebrate their birthday brought him back to when they were children. He had many regrets, but his son's treatment topped the list. The retired athletic director had not understood the importance of his son's career until he saw him on television caring for an injured player during a game. Laverne walked into the room as Michael Sr. was reminiscing on the past. "Are you okay, honey?" She asked.

"I just thought I made a mess of things. Isn't it sad that I needed to see Michael on television at the game to understand what you meant? You did try to tell me he loves football but differently. I am excited to see both again." He told his wife.

"This party will be a chance for forgiveness so we can put our family back together again. Who would have thought that Sidney and I would become such good friends? Cheer up. I am sure you will have the men back in your life soon." Laverne did her best to put a smile on her husband's face. Michael appreciated his wife's effort, but he knew it would be a long journey for him to repair his relationship with his sons. As for his feelings for Sidney, he finally grew to respect and love her.

25 FAMILY IS ALL THAT MATTERS

Saturday, October 18, was a warm day with steady winds. Laverne and Michael Sr. met Sidney at Regency Palm Country Club for a final venue walkthrough before the party. Pulling up to the front of the club, the Grayeson was impressed with the immaculate grass that was lush and green, along with the floral decorations.

Michael Sr. was scared to ask the women to visit the golf course. Rethinking the purpose of his visit, he pushed it out of his mind. After greeting the family at the glass doors, the manager explained the order of the events and the number of staff assigned to the event. The well-decorated ballroom had small blue, green, and cream color floral arrangements, with each corner consisting of two large 3 and 0 helium balloons surrounded by smaller plain balloons. The tablecloths were off-white with navy blue table runners. The ladies felt combining both men's favorite colors would show unity.

The three adults stood in the middle of the room and looked at the banquet tables, chairs, bar, and dance floor. Satisfied with the setup, they left the building to return to the hotel. Sidney's phone rang as soon as she exited the building. "Hello." She answered quickly when Larry's number appeared on the screen.

"Hi Mom, I just wanted to let you know I am at the hotel. Where are you?" Larry inquired of his mother.

"I am so glad you finally made it. I was worried I would have to attend this function by myself. I have just met with the organizers and am heading back now. I cannot wait to see you." The excited mother told her son while signaling to the Grayeson to be quiet.

Hanging up the phone, Sidney danced excitedly in front of the building. "OMG, I thought he was not going to make it. He was supposed to leave yesterday, but they called an emergency team meeting at the last minute, so he missed his flight. Then the next flight we booked ended up delaying as well. Oh man, I missed seeing that handsome face of his in person." She blurted out.

"It is so good seeing the joy you have right now. Who would have thought we would be here today?" Laverne told her.

"I cannot thank you enough for taking care of him when I could not. This celebration is as much for you both as it is for them. I love you so much. Let us go because we need to spruce ourselves up for our babies." Sidney squealed with exuberance as she hugged the couple.

They left the venue and drove to their hotels. The mothers booked different hotels to avoid Larry and Michael bumping into each other before the party. Arriving at the hotel, Laverne called her son to confirm he had also arrived in Blythe. To her amazement, he was waiting at the entrance for her.

"Hello, my favorite woman in the world." He told her.

"Hello to you too, my handsome offspring," Laverne responded.

It was the first time Michael Sr. and Michael II stood face to face in years. The greeting was quick and cold, "Dad." He stated to acknowledge him. Then wrapped his mother's hand around his arm.

Michael informed his mother of the added guest as they began walking into the hotel's lobby. "Mom, I hope you do not mind, but I invited the Gomez family to join us at the gala. I am hoping you could get them in without a problem." He held his breath, waiting for her response.

"How many Gomez arrived with you?" Laverne asked, trying to keep up appearances.

"All of them. You do not mind, do you?" He asked.

"I am sure we will be able to find a table for them. Don't worry about it.

The night is about giving back, and who is better at giving back than Ashley and Tomás. I am glad they are here. I raised such a thoughtful son. I love you, honey." Laverne smiled at the exchange and kissed her son on the cheek before returning to her room.

As she stepped into the elevator, Michael yelled, "see you in the lobby at 6:30 pm."

"Make it 6:00 pm because we must get there at 6:30 pm." She yelled back.

Michael Sr. felt like an outsider in his family as he watched the exchange between his wife and son. His exclusion hurt, and he finally understood how young Michael had felt all those years ago when he would focus on Larry and not him. "I must make amends with my son." He mumbled.

"What was that?" Laverne asked, hearing him mumbling because she did not listen to what he said.

"Nothing. Just running through the speech in my head." He told her.

"Are you sure you want to make a speech in front of everybody? It could be haphazard with your history regarding those boys." She told him.

He agreed with his wife as he inhaled and exhaled but felt it had to happen that night. They began reminiscing about when their son was younger, moving away from the topic. It lightened the mood in the hotel room, which was what they needed.

Later in the evening, everyone began gathering at the clubhouse around 6:00 pm. Dr. Gomez invented a story about his wife's shopping to arrive ahead of Michael. Around 5:45 pm, the elevator door opened, and Michael II exited wearing a well-tailored gray tweed two-button style peaky blinders suit with a white shirt and burgundy tie. He confidently walked into the lobby, drawing the women's attention to him.

Already in a relationship with Ruby, the stares and gestures did not affect Michael. He stood waiting for his mother with one hand in his pocket and one hand placed on his chest. The second elevator door opened, and he was astonished to see how gorgeous his mother looked in her off-the-shoulder silver floor-sweeping lace gown. His father's black suit complimented her dress nicely. The family members embraced each other before leaving the hotel.

At the same time, Larry wore a custom tailor-made gray three-piece suit he helped design with his friend Charmaine. Sidney also wore a customized alter yellow free-flowing floor-length dress designed for her. The upcoming designer felt proud they were wearing her first men's suit and woman's gown. Exiting the elevator, Sidney looked radiant with an upswept hairstyle. The mother and son embraced each other before walking out to the hired car waiting for them.

The mothers hired two cars to drive both families to the venue as part of the charade. Sidney and Laverne planned for the vehicles to pick up each family member at the hotels to arrive at the country club simultaneously. The driver closed the door behind his passengers after the Grayeson family entered the vehicle and immediately radioed the other driver to leave the hotel. Both drivers traveled the planned route to avoid ruining the surprise upon receiving the confirmation.

Sidney contacted the banquet manager to ensure no one was near the window as they approached the venue. The manager told the guests to stand against the back wall, and the DJ began playing instrumental music to continue the gala charade. Sidney's car arrived first and drove to the north entrance of the building. A few minutes later, Laverne's car went to the south end. A member of the banquet team met both families and escorted them into the room simultaneously. As soon as they entered, everyone yelled, "Surprise."

Larry and Michael looked across the room at each other. The two men looked shocked and bewildered at first. Each turned to their mothers, hugged them, then met in the middle of the room. It was the first time both had been in the same room on their birthday.

Completing the pleasantries, Laverne called out, "let the party begin," to the guest. The DJ began playing the song selections from the hosts as people were still moving around the room and socializing.

"Hello, hello, can everyone be quiet for a moment, please?" The voice came over the speaker to grab the guests' attention. The guests quieted down and found their seats.

"Thank you all for coming to celebrate my Larry and Michael's 30th birthday. The journey to get here was not easy, but these men pushed through, and here we are. Aren't they handsome?" Sidney asked the crowd.

Many of the guests replied in agreement. Stretching her left hand, she asked Laverne to join her at the microphone. "Family, friends, and the in-between, none of this would be possible without this beautiful and amazing woman standing next to me. Mrs. Laverne Grayeson is Michael's mother and will forever be Larry's foster mother. She cared for my son as her own until I could, and I am eternally grateful for that. Since she is my cohort in tricking these men into joining us for their party, I know she would like to say something." Sidney handed the microphone to Laverne.

"Good evening, everyone, and as Sidney said, thank you all for coming. Pulling a surprise party off for these two men, I can say that

because they might not speak to me if I call them babies in public."
She laughed.

The crowd laughed with her as Michael and Larry nodded in
agreement.

"All that you see here would not have happened if either of them
caught wind of the party. We had to produce plausible stories to get
them to leave their cities, jobs, and hobbies so we could celebrate them.
Many of you want to wish them a happy birthday, but we would like
to do that after feeding you. The banquet manager will call out your
tables; please move quickly, so the buffet line does not become a traffic
jam. Before we all run to the food, I would like to ask Minister
Hopewell to say grace." Laverne told the guest, then handed the mic
to the minister.

Minister Hopewell smiled as he stood before his friend's guests.
"Don't worry; it won't be a long prayer." He told them. Once the
chuckles died down, he began, "Heavenly Father, thank you for the
safe journey for all in attendance today. As we celebrate the birth of
your sons, Larry and Michael, I ask you to help them enjoy the
birthday festivities tonight with their guests. Now, Lord, please bless
the meal so it can bring nourishment to our bodies. Bless the hands
that prepared the meal so they can prosper. In Jesus' name. Amen.
Let's eat."

The hungry guests were in good spirits as the coordinator called
their table numbers. The lines moved fast because Laverne requested
two banquet stations with the same meal. Larry, Michael, and their
families sat at the long table. The table included the guest of honors,
their parents, Martin, Ruby, and Rosalind, Larry's girlfriend. No one
was surprised to see Martin because Larry discovered the truth about
his mother and her constant visitor when he was twenty-five years old.
He was angry at first, but he accepted Martin to a degree after hearing
the full story.

Laughter around the room was infectious. Michael Sr. knew it was
not the time to express his sorrow in front of strangers. Immediately
following dinner, he pulled his wife aside to ask for her help.
"Sweetie, you are right. It is not the time or place to make a grand
speech. However, I still want to make peace with my boys. Can you
help me? If you could get them to meet me outside, I can take it from
there. It's clear that if I ask, they will say no."

Laverne, taking pity on her husband, spotted Larry and Michael close to one another. Walking over to Michael first, she placed her hand around his arms and asked for a moment of his time. She then did the same to Larry. "I am so proud of you both. You have done well for yourselves, but you both have some unfinished business, and I think it is time you all resolve it." She told them while escorting them out of the room onto the back patio.

His mother's attempt to resolve an issue became clear when he saw his father standing there. Michael II's first instinct was to walk away; however, he sensed from his mother's comment that it was time to have the conversation or listen. Larry was not as accommodating as Michael, but with persuasion from Laverne, he returned to the patio.

Michael Sr. cleared his throat before expressing his feelings, "first, I want to apologize to you both for my behavior. My tunnel vision of being a football star made me try to force my dreams on you. I am not making excuses for my actions because it was appalling, and I am extremely ashamed of myself." Pausing for a minute, he waited to see if one of them would respond. When neither replied, he continued.

"Michael, I treated you poorly because I could not understand how anyone could love football and not play the game. When Larry said he wanted to play, I felt like I got another chance at football. Larry, you are talented, and I truly consider you my son. I am sorry I tried to live through you and caused you to lose your closeness with Michael. Nothing I can say will erase what I did, but I hope we can start again. Can you both forgive me? I miss my boys." Michael Sr. held his breath while waiting for one of them to speak.

Larry looked at Michael Sr. and Michael II, then walked closer to younger Michael, "daddy Michael, what you did was foul, but I am just as guilty. When I was younger, I was desperate for a father figure, and I took advantage of your love for football. I would also like to apologize to you, Michael. I miss how close we were when I first started living with you before football got in the way. Can we have our relationship back?" He asked, leaning against the white column.

The music echoed into the hallway, along with laughter from the guests. Michael II wished his father would acknowledge him and apologize for his actions in the past. It became a reality, yet it did not have the same meaning to him. Dr. Michael II realized he no longer required any apology to make life better for himself. He appreciated Larry and his father's words highlighting how they felt, but it was unnecessary. Smiling, "I accepted your apologies long ago, even before you spoke it. It is all good." he mentioned, then returned to the party.

The remaining men stood in the hallway, uncertain of the next action. Michael Sr. patted Larry on the shoulder as they walked back into the party. The relationship would not be as before, but they hoped it could be a new beginning.

The DJ began playing dance music and encouraged the guests to join each other on the dance floor. Ruby walked into the middle of the dance floor and motioned to Michael to join her. Although the moment was not what he planned, he would take the opportunity to propose. Joining her, they danced for a few minutes; Michael got down on one knee when she turned her back. Dr. Gomez, who was watching the couple, told the DJ to stop the music when he saw Michael positioning to propose. Ruby saw Michael on his knee when she turned to complain about the music interruption.

"Ruby Adrianne Gomez, from the moment I saw you walk down the stairs, you set my heart on fire. You waited for me to complete my education and internship throughout the years without ever pressuring or questioning my commitment. Would you make me the happiest man alive and agree to marry me? Will you be my wife?"

Tears flowed down the young woman's face as she placed both hands over her mouth in astonishment. There were times when she wondered if they would ever get married. Now the man of her dreams is saying the words she waited to hear. "Oh, Michael, you have no idea how long I have waited for this; yes, of course, I'll marry you." She turned and looked for her parents, then back at Michael.

The couple received warm wishes from their families and guests. Laverne recognized the surprise and joy on Ashley's face when she glanced over. The women met in the middle of the floor to wish their children well.

Dr. Gomez and Michael Sr. stepped outside to smoke a cigar to celebrate the news. Larry embraced his foster brother and expressed how happy he was for them. Rosalind, who met the family for the first time, was jealous it was not her. Taking note of Michael's comment about his girlfriend not applying pressure, she offered congratulations and then remained quiet.

As the night winded down to an end, Dr. Michael and Larry decided to speak to the guest before they left the venue, "thank you all for coming and making this milestone birthday extremely memorable. We both appreciate each of you, so please enjoy the party and have a safe journey home or wherever you are going after this." Michael handed the phone to Larry, "exactly what he said. Thank you, everyone. DJ, turn the music up."

It was not instantaneous, but Michael Sr. could finally enjoy time with his sons. He traveled to games across the country courtesy of Dr. Michael and Larry. Michael and Ruby were married in Los Angeles a year after the proposal, around his birthday in October. To the dismay of the couple, the wedding was glamorous and expensive. Ashley and Laverne began planning the wedding as soon as they left the birthday party. They consulted with Ruby on the wedding venue, meal, and color scheme. Ruby, who hated planning, welcomed the women's agreement to host the event. Dr. Michael consulted with Larry's friend to design his suit and his fiancé's wedding dress. Traveling to the games left little time for the groom-to-be to attend fittings, so it was up to Larry, the best man, to arrange them.

During one of those quick trips, Larry discussed his intentions to marry his girlfriend. "Bro, would it be tacky if I propose to Rosalind at the end of your wedding? I don't want to take away from your big day." Michael felt good that his brother was asking permission, but he knew it was unnecessary. "That is the perfect time to ask, especially since she will not be expecting it. She compliments you perfectly, and I am so happy for you. Don't worry; I won't tell anyone, not even Ruby. Since the birthday party, both ladies have been like two peas in a pod." Dr. Michael told him.

The planning and coordination went smoothly, and Larry proposed to Rosalind, to her surprise, at the end of the wedding reception. Her only regret was that her parents were not in attendance to see the proposal. The family looked forward to planning another wedding and, hopefully, a baby shower. Larry and Michael II vowed to learn from Michael Sr. whenever they have children. Michael Sr. was determined to improve as he moved forward with his retirement and family.

26 DON'T MAKE MY MISTAKE

As time passed for Michael Grayeson Sr., he began instructing other fathers about using the right words in conversations with their children. It was during one of his sessions when a young father approached him. The man was upset about his son's choice of ballet versus sports. This uncomfortable conversation allowed Michael Sr. to provide insights into his life to the younger father. Afterward, the older man had to establish if the issue was the boy's career choice or what he feared his lifestyle would be. The young man quickly assured him of his concerns, "I am not worried about his lifestyle choices; I don't want him to lose the opportunity to go to college on a scholarship. His mom and I tried to provide the best we could, but we did not have money saved for his education. That is why he must be great at something to get into school. I cannot watch him work in a dead-end job day in and day out that barely pays any money like me." Mitchell told Mr. Grayeson.

His concern brought the older man back to his conversation with his wife about choosing to go with Larry to his football tryouts. He disguised his true feelings behind the need for the boy to get a scholarship. Using wisdom, he responded, "Does your son love sports or ballet?"

"What kind of a question is that?" Mitchell asked, trying to keep his emotions from escalating.

"My question may seem strange, but it will make sense once you answer." Mr. Grayeson told him after recognizing the anger Mitchell felt at the question.

"What does it matter what he loves. I need him to go to college to have a better future." The distraught father told him.

Shaking his head, the older man spoke honestly to the young father. "See, that is where you are wrong. It does matter what he loves. If you want him to excel in life, it is best if he progresses in what he loves." Mitchell grunted at the suggestion that his son's future would be anything but disastrous if he chose what he loves. Mr. Grayeson knew he had to find a way to get the father to focus on his son's abilities, not what he felt was right. "Have you seen him play?" He asked.

"Yes, of course, I watched him play. He is all right, but he could get better with enough practice." The father told him.

"Have you watched him dance?" Mr. Grayeson realized the question could be tricky, yet he continued to ask.

Mitchell looked at the older man in disbelief. "Why would I watch him throw his life away? He has no future prancing around a stage for little or no money. How would that make me a good father encouraging him to do that?" He asked him.

Mr. Grayeson rose from his chair and walked to the window. Talking to the young father was reminiscent of when his wife used to try to get through to him. His mind was wrapped up with only football in the past, leaving him no room for anything else. It caused him to lose sight of what was important to his family. Although Mitchell's focus is not sports, his determination to get his son a scholarship has blinded him to his son's talents. Michael knew he had to shift his tactics when dealing with Mitchell.

Walking back to the table, he asked a different question. "What is your son's name, and where does he attend school?"

The question jarred the young father. "My son's name is Clifford, and he attends Cooper High School. What does that have to do with the conversation?" He responded in an icy tone.

"It might be nothing or might be everything. One second." Keeping up on technology, Michael took out his phone and searched for the school. Once he found the website, he searched the department listing and found the drama club. Holding his breath, he prayed they had videos of performances and for Clifford to be in one of them. Luckily, the drama club had a list of cast members on the site. Carefully strolling through the videos, he found two with Clifford Brown listed as a performer. Instinctively he clicked play on the video marked 'Changing Faces.'

Mr. Grayeson handed the phone to the father and instructed him to watch it. Reluctantly Mitchell watched the video of his son. Minutes into the performance, he saw the young man come alive on the stage. It looks as though he had light beaming from the inside out. Tears began to roll down the man's face. He could not believe how effortless dancing was for his son. At the end of the video, he sent the link to his phone before handing it back to Michael.

"Wow, he's good, but how will that get him into college?" Mitchell asked rhetorically.

"Look, if that is what he wants to do, he will find the school and the scholarship to get him there. You must trust your son's ability and stop resisting the path he is carving for himself. I am not sure if you are a believing man, but in the bible, somewhere in the Proverbs, it says your gift will make room for you. If your son shows the passion and love I saw in the short clip, he should have no problem finding an art school that will give him a scholarship.

My suggestion is to sit down and have an honest conversation with him. When you do, make sure you hear his heart's desire and not any preconceived response."

Mitchell realized that he was imposing his desires on his son and not allowing his son to express his feelings. At the end of the conversation, Mitchell agreed to talk with his son. Michael felt pleased that he could help a man in a similar position as he was.

His sessions started as a one-off and turned into a monthly profitable vocation. He spoke on various pitfalls parents make when it comes to their children and even their spouses. At the end of every session, he would tell those in attendance, "It is never simple living in the shadow of anyone, so make those you love the center stage when possible. Your belief is just that, "your belief," and not necessarily theirs."

Words we can all live by as we grow older.

ABOUT THE AUTHOR

Paulette Bernard, a graduate of the University of Phoenix, obtained her Master of Technology, Research and Development Degree and her Bachelor of Computer Technology at DeVry's University; find solace in words. Her earliest memory of writing started from an early age when she was in elementary school, and her love kept increasing. Her imaginative and creative path stems from her inability to fit in with the crowds or popular kids. As she grew, so did her craft of writing which she used to write special messages for her friends, family members, and co-workers. Her love of writing, traveling, and her vivid imagination made it natural for her to create the stories her readers have grown to love. She published her first book, *Love's Voyage*, in 2010, and as a resident of Georgia, she continues to search for ideas, and her search has led to many works waiting to be published.

www.ingramcontent.com/pod-product-compliance
Lightning Source LLC
Chambersburg PA
CBHW070605180626
46817CB00005B/1998